W9-DES-860

BISON
BOOKS

Spreading his powerful wings, he rose, while Duare stretched her hands toward me.

Pirates of Venus

Edgar Rice Burroughs

INTRODUCTION TO THE BISON BOOKS EDITION BY
F. Paul Wilson

AFTERWORD BY PHILLIP R. BURGER

GLOSSARY BY SCOTT TRACY GRIFFIN

FRONTISPIECE BY J. ALLEN ST. JOHN

ILLUSTRATIONS BY THOMAS FLOYD

University of Nebraska Press
Lincoln and London

Manufactured in the United States of America
∞
First Bison Books printing: 2001

Library of Congress Cataloging-in-Publication Data
Burroughs, Edgar Rice, 1875–1950.
Pirates of Venus / by Edgar Rice Burroughs ; frontispiece by J. Allen St. John ; illustrations by Thomas Floyd ; introduction to the Bison Books ed. by F. Paul Wilson ; afterword by Phillip R. Burger ; glossary by Scott Tracy Griffin.—Commemorative ed.
p. cm.—(Bison frontiers of imagination series)
ISBN 0-8032-6183-7 (pbk.: alk. paper)
1. Venus (Planet)—Fiction. I. Title. II. Bison frontiers of imagination.
PS3503.U687 P57 2001
813'.52—dc21 2001027712

CONTENTS

F. PAUL WILSON

Introduction

The serial version of *Pirates of Venus* began its six-issue run in *Argosy Weekly* in 1932. At the time, Edgar Rice Burroughs appeared to have the world by the tale.

Consider: MGM's *Tarzan the Ape Man*, the first Tarzan talkie, starring Maureen O'Sullivan and an Olympic swimmer named Johnny Weissmuller, was well on its way to becoming one of the most popular and profitable movies of the year. Burroughs's publishing venture, ERB Inc., had just released its third title (*Tarzan Triumphant*) and, despite dire warnings that he would be courting disaster by self-publishing, was turning a profit. The Tarzan daily comic strip illustrated by Rex Maxon was syndicated in more than 250 newspapers, and the brilliant Hal Foster, who later created Prince Valiant, had started illustrating the color Sunday page. The Tarzan radio show had just debuted, sparking, via its sponsors, a surge of merchandising that encompassed everything from Tarzan statuettes and spears to Tarzan chewing gum. In addition to his ranch, he had a new beachfront home in Malibu. The town of Tarzana, named after his ranch, had been incorporated, designated with its own postmark.

But typical of Burroughs's life, every silver lining had its cloud. Never satisfied with the considerable income from his writing, he had spent the preceding decade looking for ways to parlay that money into even larger profits. In one venture he had converted part of the Tarzana ranch into the El Caballero Country Club, which recently had gone into default and foreclosure. Apache Motors, an airplane engine company he'd underwritten, had failed, taking his entire investment with it. He'd had a recent run of medical problems, requiring multiple surgical procedures for bladder obstruction. And to top it all off, his marriage was crumbling.

In spite of all this, Edgar Rice Burroughs, at age fifty-seven, was in one of the more productive periods of his writing life, having completed seven novels, a half-dozen murder-mystery shorts, a novella, and sundry articles in a two-and-one-half-year period. After finishing a pair of back-to-back Tarzan novels (*The Triumph of Tarzan* and *Tarzan and the City of Gold*), he decided to invent a fresh landscape for a new series of adventures. He already had conquered Africa, the earth's core, various lost continents, and Mars, so he turned his eye toward the morning star, Venus.

Otis Adelbert Kline, ERB's most successful imitator, already had swashbuckled Venus with *Planet of Peril* and *Prince of Peril*, but that didn't deter Burroughs; neither did the current scientific evidence about the planet.

We know now from the Magellan, Mariner, and Venera missions that the clouds wreathing the second planet consist of concentrated sulfuric acid droplets, and the atmosphere below is carbon dioxide with a fairly uniform temperature in excess of 700 kelvin, or 860 degrees Fahrenheit. The photos sent back from the missions show a bleak, barren surface. But even in the 1930s when Burroughs began his Venus adventures, most astronomers had declared the planet an inhospitable world. Sir James Jeans, one of the most respected cosmologists of the day, postulated that although the atmosphere might contain a little oxygen, there was by no means enough to sustain higher life forms.

Undaunted, Burroughs set his sights on Venus and began spinning his tales.

At first glance *Pirates of Venus* and its sequels might appear to be a rehash of the John Carter Mars novels. Not so. Burroughs's Venus novels have their own distinct character, in both their tone and their protagonist, Carson Napier. When one looks at what was happening in Burroughs's life at the time, it's plain that Carson Napier, much more so than John Carter, Tarzan, or David Innes, was a conscious reflection of his creator.

True to the Burroughs formula, Carson Napier is a wealthy, capable man of good family (like John Carter, Virginian blood flows in his veins; like Tarzan, he can learn a new language in three weeks). He's also brash and impulsive, and he doesn't always think things through as carefully as he should. (In a later story Carson says, "I must be the prize incompetent of two worlds.") He finds himself on Venus by trying to rocket to Mars: he builds a giant torpedo in Mexico, aims it at Mars (not where Mars will be when he reaches its orbit, but directly at that little red dot as it rises above the horizon), and shoots himself into space. He hasn't accounted for the moon's gravitational pull, and it's not long before he's headed straight toward a fiery death in the sun. Fortunately the planet Venus gets in his way and he parachutes to safety. (Well, relative safety, since no one is safe for long in a Burroughs tale.)

This creates a motif for the rest of the novel and for the entire Venus series as well. Unlike Tarzan or John Carter, who always seem to be in control, or who, when presented with a new set of dangerous circumstances, soon have the situation well in hand, Carson seems to be playing by ear, and at times he appears to be tone deaf. Most of Burroughs's heroes *make* things happen, but things tend to happen *to* Carson Napier.

The novel's wry tone is set in the opening chapter, which offers a glimpse not only into the offices of ERB Inc., but into the life of the author as well. As narrator of the chapter, Burroughs never mentions himself by name, but he does name and converse with his real-life amanuensis, Ralph Rothmund. He mentions being distracted by "the annoying details of a real-estate transaction that was going wrong." And when the narrator has what he thinks is a hallucination, Rothmund repeats a warning about the aftereffects of the narcotics taken during the course of his "last operation." No question about it, Burroughs is venting his workaday concerns in front of his readership. (But not necessarily his true character. He tells Napier, "I detest business and everything connected with it." Odd statement from a writer known to challenge publishers' word counts and haggle over a quarter-cent in word rates; a man in the process of building an empire out of his literary properties.)

The purpose of the opener, as in so many of Burroughs's novels, is to assure readers that what they are about to read is true and to establish a rationale for how the author has learned of the extraordinary exploits related in the pages that follow (a hoary Victorian conceit that Burroughs used time and again). In it Carson Napier, born of a British father and an American mother in India, where he learned certain mystic arts, demonstrates his ability to speak to Burroughs's mind and to project telepathic images (which makes one wonder if ERB had been tuning in to that hot new radio drama, *The Shadow*). Carson wants someone "of sufficient intelligence and culture" with "a reputation for integrity" to relate the details of his trip to Mars. As mentioned previously, he lands on Venus instead. Nevertheless he contacts the author telepathically across the tens of millions of miles to recount his adventures. Thus Napier tells Burroughs, Burroughs repeats the story into his Dictaphone (he was dictating most of his fiction at this time), after which the account is transcribed by Rothmund, who sends it on to the publisher.

We follow Carson as he bails out of his torpedo and plummets through the planet's double layer of clouds until his parachute snags on a branch of one of the giant trees of Amtor, as the natives call the planet. The trunks of these trees can reach one thousand feet in diameter as they soar many thousands of feet into the clouds. They're home to a race of civilized humans known as the Vepajan, who have carved their dwellings into the boles of the trees. After rescuing Carson from a one-eyed, lobster-clawed predator, the Vepajans take him in and teach him their language.

During his schooling Carson learns that because of their planet's perpetual cloud cover the natives have no concept of astronomy. They believe Amtor to be a huge disk afloat on a sea of molten metal and rock. Near the rim of the disk is Strabol, the hot country (what we'd call the equator); Karbol, one of the poles, is the circular cold country at the center of the disk; and Trabol, the temperate country, where most of the population lives, lies between the two extremes. Since no one has crossed the hot country and survived, the Vepajans have no evidence to contradict their floating-disk theory and cannot conceive of a spherical world. In one of the novel's more humorous exchanges, Burroughs takes an amiable swipe at Einstein as Carson's Vepajan teacher explains away obvious inherent discrepancies in the maps of Amtor by invoking the great scientist Klufar's "theory of relativity of distance."

Burroughs used the Amtor setting to explore a theme that must have been especially attractive at this point in his life: immortality. He was looking his sixtieth birthday in the eye, he'd been hospitalized recently for an obstructed bladder, and a younger woman, Florence Dearholt, soon to be the second Mrs. Burroughs, had caught his eye. Perhaps as a result of all this he made the Vepajans virtually immortal, not because of a genetic trait or an effect of the planet itself, but due to a serum they had perfected a thousand years before. It was not merely an anti-aging preparation, but a protectant from disease as well. They offer Carson a dose and he accepts. Burroughs no doubt longed for the same opportunity.

But Carson soon discovers that Amtor is not quite the Garden of Eden it appears to be. He learns that the island nation of Vepaja is at war with the Thorists. Long ago, it seems, the Vepajan society occupied a huge territory, but they were a stratified monarchic society. A group of dissidents calling themselves Thorists engineered a revolt by promising the lower classes "no masters, no taxes, no laws." But after a bloody revolution that sent the decimated upper classes into exile, the masses discovered they'd been duped into "exchanging the beneficent rule of an experienced and cultured class for that of greedy incompetents and theorists."

It requires no profound exegesis to read Marxists for Thorists, especially if you're familiar with Burroughs's politics. Conservative doesn't quite do justice to his place on the Left-Right spectrum. Perhaps a couple sentences from *Pirates of Venus* will lend a better idea. At this point in the story Carson has been fomenting rebellion among his fellow captives on a Thorist prison ship; his rebel group calls itself the Soldiers of Liberty. "[Kiron] did not say Soldier of Liberty, but "kung, kung, kung," which are the Amtorian initials of the order's title. Kung is the name of the Amtorian character that represents the K sound in our language, and when I first translated the initials I was compelled to smile at the similarity they bore to those of a well-known secret order in the United States of America." This is not to say that he was a card-carrying fascist, because many of his novels skewer dictatorships of all stripes with equal relish, but his views were unquestionably well right of center.

Even if Burroughs had been a more liberal sort, his depiction of the Thorists as villains might simply have reflected what he had read in his daily papers. Russia in the early 1930s had been wracked by one famine after another, millions in the Ukraine were dying of starvation, and its infrastructure lay in ruins; it was about to embark on its second Five-Year Plan, which no one expected to be any more successful than the first. Clearly the Bolsheviks had botched it.

So had the Thorists. The egalitarian society they'd promised never came to be; instead, their people lived under the iron fist of a military dictatorship, with spies everywhere to ferret out anyone who might be plotting a counterrevolution. In our first look at a group of Thorists, they are described by Carson as "coarser, more brutal" than any Vepajans he has seen. The individuals in question have invaded the tree kingdom to kidnap the beautiful princess living next door to Carson. Why? It seems that during the revolution, the Thorist zealots killed or drove out the best and the brightest of the old order. The long-term effects of this brain drain have caused their society to deteriorate to the point where they must abduct Vepajans, not only to update their scientific knowledge but to upgrade their gene pool as well.

Which opens another door in the Edgar Rice Burroughs psyche: welcome to the Eugenics Suite.

For years Burroughs had been an outspoken proponent of eugenics, a philosophy advocating the forced sterilization of criminals and "mental defectives." It was around the time he was writing the early Venus novels that he penned an essay called "I See a New Race." It envisions an America of the future where peace and prosperity reign because for generations "criminals, defectives, and incompetents" have been sterilized, thus removing their "tainted" genes from the population. He never found a publisher for it.

In *Pirates of Venus* Burroughs dipped his toes in the eugenics pool, but he took a swan dive into the deep end with the sequel, *Lost on Venus*, which strands Carson and the Princess Duare in Havatoo, a society governed entirely by the principles of eugenics.

By the time Burroughs died in 1950, the Venus series totaled four volumes—*Pirates of Venus, Lost on Venus, Carson of Venus,* and *Escape on Venus*—but they read like one very long novel, each taking up where the other has left off. This can be frustrating because the books have no conclusion. The last page of *Pirates of Venus* leaves Carson facing certain capture by the Thorists; he may be happy in the knowledge that the Princess Duare returns his love, but none of the plot lines is resolved. Readers were not kept long in suspense, however. The first installment of *Lost on Venus*—already written by the time *Pirates of Venus* saw print—appeared a few months later in the 4 March 1933 issue of the same magazine, *Argosy Weekly. Lost on Venus* rejoins Carson Napier only minutes after the close of *Pirates of Venus* and, thankfully, provides some closure, with Carson flying the Princess Duare back toward Vepaja in a homemade plane. (The no-conclusion problem was remedied temporarily in 1963 when Dover Books reprinted *Pirates of Venus* and *Lost on Venus* in a single volume, joining the tale of Carson Napier's first few months on Venus into a continuous narrative.)

Burroughs didn't return to Venus until 1938 when *Carson of Venus* was serialized like its predecessors in *Argosy.* He was at work on the fourth Venus book in December 1941, when World War II exploded, and his role as war correspondent cut down his fiction output. *Escape on Venus* didn't see print until 1946. If you've browsed Burroughs's titles you may have seen a book called *The Wizard of Venus,* but it's not a novel. The title story is a 1941 novella that went unpublished in ERB's lifetime. In 1970 it was resurrected from a trunk and cobbled together with "Pirate Blood," an unsold eugenics broadside in story form from the 1930s.

Although it started off well, the Venus series deteriorated along the way into a succession of capture-and-escape novellas (indeed some segments were published as self-contained stories before inclusion in the books) that were strung together by the slimmest of narrative threads. But *Pirates of Venus* and *Lost on Venus* remain milestones in the Burroughs oeuvre.

You now hold the inaugural volume. Here begin the adventures of Carson Napier, Burroughs's most flawed hero and the character closest to his true self. The journey through *Pirates of Venus* is an excursion through the author's head. So let's not waste any more time . . .

AMTOR
SCALE MIS 0 1000 2000 3000 4000 5000
VOLAP
NOR
VODARO
ATOR
MOLIS
SMALL CIRCLE
OCEAN
ANLAP
DONUK
KOOAAD
TRAMBOL
LEPAJ
OMBAJ
HALPI
OCEAN
ANDOO
STRABOL
KORMOR
MOROV
GANTA ISLAND
ZANDO
NOOBOL
KAPDOR
TRABOL
KARBOL
GREAT CIRCLE
VAXLAP
OCEAN
THORA

Pirates of Venus

CHAPTER ONE

Carson Napier

"If a female figure in a white shroud enters your bedchamber at midnight on the thirteenth day of this month, answer this letter; otherwise, do not."

Having read this far in the letter, I was about to consign it to the wastebasket, where all my crank letters go; but for some reason I read on, "If she speaks to you, please remember her words and repeat them to me when you write." I might have read on to the end; but at this juncture the telephone bell rang, and I dropped the letter into one of the baskets on my desk. It chanced to be the "out" basket; and had events followed their ordinary course, this would have been the last of the letter and the incident in so far as I was concerned, for from the "out" basket the letter went to the files.

It was Jason Gridley on the telephone. He seemed excited and asked me to come to his laboratory at once. As Jason is seldom excited about anything, I hastened to accede to his request and satisfy my curiosity. Jumping into my roadster, I soon covered the few blocks that separate us, to learn that Jason had good grounds for excitement. He had just received a radio message from the inner world, from Pellucidar.

On the eve of the departure of the great dirigible, O–220, from the earth's core, following the successful termination of that historic expedition, Jason had determined to remain and search for von Horst, the only missing member of the party; but Tarzan, David Innes, and Captain Zuppner had persuaded him of the folly of such an undertaking, inasmuch as David had promised to dispatch an expedition of his own native Pellucidarian warriors to locate the young German lieutenant if he still lived and it were possible to discover any clue to his whereabouts.

Notwithstanding this, and though he had returned to the outer world with the ship, Jason had always been harassed by a sense of responsibility for the fate of von Horst, a young man who had been most popular with all the members of the expedition; and had insisted time and time again that he regretted having left Pellucidar until he had exhausted every means within his power of rescuing von Horst or learned definitely that he was dead.

Jason waved me to a chair and offered me a cigarette. "I've just had a message from Abner Perry," he announced, "the first for months."

"It must have been interesting," I commented, "to excite *you.*"

"It was," he admitted. "A rumor has reached Sari that von Horst has been found."

Now as this pertains to a subject entirely foreign to the present volume, I might mention that I have alluded to it only for the purpose of explaining two facts which, while not vital, have some slight bearing on the remarkable sequence of events which followed. First, it caused me to forget the letter I just mentioned, and, second, it fixed the date in my mind—the tenth.

My principal reason for mentioning the first fact is to stress the thought that the matter of the letter, so quickly and absolutely forgotten, had no opportunity to impress itself upon my mind and therefore could not, at least objectively, influence my consideration of ensuing events. The letter was gone from my mind within five minutes of its reading as completely as though it had never been received.

The next three days were exceedingly busy ones for me, and when I retired on the night of the thirteenth my mind was so filled with the annoying details of a real estate transaction that was going wrong, that it was some time before I could sleep. I can truthfully affirm that my last thoughts were of trust deeds, receivers in equity, and deficiency judgments.

What awoke me, I do not know. I sat up with a start just in time to see a female figure, swathed in what appeared to be a white winding sheet, enter my room through the door. You will note that I say door rather than doorway, for such was the fact; the door was closed. It was a clear, moonlit night; the various homely objects in my room were plainly discernible, especially the ghostly figure now hovering near the foot of my bed.

I am not subject to hallucinations, I had never seen a ghost, I had never wished to, and I was totally ignorant of the ethics governing such a situation. Even had the lady not been so obviously supernatural, I should yet have been at a loss as to how to receive her at this hour in the intimacy of my bedchamber, for no strange lady had ever before invaded its privacy, and I am of Puritan stock.

"It is midnight of the thirteenth," she said, in a low, musical voice.

"So it is," I agreed, and then I recalled the letter that I had received on the tenth.

"He left Guadalupe today," she continued; "he will wait in Guaymas for your letter."

That was all. She crossed the room and passed out of it, not through the window which was quite convenient, but through the solid wall. I sat there for a full minute, staring at the spot where I had last seen her and endeavoring to convince myself that I was dreaming, but I was not dreaming; I was wide awake. In fact I was so wide awake that it was fully an hour before I had successfully wooed Morpheus, as the Victorian writers so neatly expressed it, ignoring the fact that his sex must have made it rather embarrassing for gentlemen writers.

I reached my office a little earlier than usual the following morning, and it is needless to say that the first thing that I did was to search for that letter which I had received on the tenth. I could recall neither the name of the writer nor the point of origin of the letter, but my secretary recalled the latter, the letter having been sufficiently out of the ordinary to attract his attention.

"It was from somewhere in Mexico," he said, and as letters of this nature are filed by states and countries, there was now no difficulty in locating it.

You may rest assured that this time I read the letter carefully. It was dated the third and postmarked Guaymas. Guaymas is a seaport in Sonora, on the Gulf of California.

Here is the letter:

> My dear Sir:
>
> Being engaged in a venture of great scientific importance, I find it necessary to solicit the assistance (not financial) of some one psychologically harmonious, who is at the same time of sufficient intelligence and culture to appreciate the vast possibilities of my project.
>
> Why I have addressed you I shall be glad to explain in the happy event that a personal interview seems desirable. This can only be ascertained by a test which I shall now explain.
>
> If a female figure in a white shroud enters your bedchamber at midnight on the thirteenth day of this month, answer this letter; otherwise, do not. If she speaks to you, please remember her words and repeat them to me when you write.
>
> Assuring you of my appreciation of your earnest consideration of this letter, which I realize is rather unusual, and begging that you hold its contents in strictest confidence until future events shall have warranted its publication, I am, Sir,
>
> Very respectfully yours,
>
> CARSON NAPIER.

"It looks to me like another nut," commented Rothmund.

"So it did to me on the tenth," I agreed; "but today is the fourteenth, and now it looks like another story."

"What has the fourteenth got to do with it?" he demanded.

"Yesterday was the thirteenth," I reminded him.

"You don't mean to tell me—" he started, skeptically.

"That is just what I do mean to tell you," I interrupted. "The lady came, I saw, she conquered."

Ralph looked worried. "Don't forget what your nurse told you after your last operation," he reminded me.

"Which nurse? I had nine, and no two of them told me the same things."

"Jerry. She said that narcotics often affected a patient's mind for months afterward." His tone was solicitous.

"Well, at least Jerry admitted that I had a mind, which some of the others didn't. Anyway, it didn't affect my eyesight; I saw what I saw. Please take a letter to Mr. Napier."

A few days later I received a telegram from Napier dated Guaymas.

"LETTER RECEIVED STOP THANKS STOP SHALL CALL ON YOU TOMORROW," it read.

"He must be flying," I commented.

"Or coming in a white shroud," suggested Ralph. "I think I'll phone Captain Hodson to send a squad car around here; sometimes these nuts are dangerous." He was still skeptical.

I must admit that we both awaited the arrival of Carson Napier with equal interest. I think Ralph expected to see a wild-eyed maniac. I could not visualize the man at all.

About eleven o'clock the following morning Ralph came into my study. "Mr. Napier is here," he said.

"Does his hair grow straight out from his scalp, and do the whites of his eyes show all around the irises?" I inquired, smiling.

"No," replied Ralph, returning the smile; "he is a very fine looking man, but," he added, "I still think he's a nut."

"Ask him to come in," and a moment later Ralph ushered in an exceptionally handsome man whom I judged to be somewhere between twenty-five and thirty years old, though he might have been even younger.

He came forward with extended hand as I rose to greet him, a smile lighting his face; and after the usual exchange of banalities he came directly to the point of his visit.

"To get the whole picture clearly before you," he commenced, "I shall have to tell you something about myself. My father was a British army officer, my mother an American girl from Virginia. I was born in India while my father was stationed there, and brought up under the tutorage of an old Hindu who was much attached to my father and mother. This Chand Kabi was something of a mystic, and he taught me many things that are not in the curriculums of schools for boys under ten. Among them was telepathy, which he had cultivated to such a degree that he could converse with one in psychological harmony with himself quite as easily at great distances as when face to face. Not only that, but he could project mental images to great distances, so that the recipient of his thought waves could see what Chand Kabi was seeing, or whatever else Chand Kabi wished him to see. These things he taught me."

"And it was thus you caused me to see my midnight visitor on the thirteenth?" I inquired.

He nodded. "That test was necessary in order to ascertain if we were in psychological harmony. Your letter, quoting the exact words that I had caused the apparition to appear to speak, convinced me that I had at last found the person for whom I have been searching for some time.

"But to get on with my story. I hope I am not boring you, but I feel that it is absolutely necessary that you should have full knowledge of my antecedents and background in order that you may decide whether I am worthy of your confidence and assistance, or not." I assured him that I was far from being bored, and he proceeded.

"I was not quite eleven when my father died and my mother brought me to America. We went to Virginia first and lived there for three years with my mother's grandfather, Judge John Carson, with whose name and reputation you are doubtless familiar, as who is not?

"After the grand old man died, mother and I came to California, where I attended public schools and later entered a small college at Claremont, which is noted for its high scholastic standing and the superior personnel of both its faculty and student body.

"Shortly after my graduation the third and greatest tragedy of my life occurred—my mother died. I was absolutely stunned by this blow. Life seemed to hold no further interest for me. I did not care to live, yet I would not take my own life. As an alternative I embarked upon a life of recklessness. With a certain goal in mind, I learned to fly. I changed my name and became a stunt man in pictures.

"I did not have to work. Through my mother I had inherited a considerable fortune from my great-grandfather, John Carson; so great a fortune that only a spendthrift could squander the income. I mention this only because the venture I am undertaking requires considerable capital, and I wish you to know that I am amply able to finance it without help.

"Not only did life in Hollywood bore me, but here in Southern California were too many reminders of the loved one I had lost. I determined to travel, and I did. I flew all over the world. In Germany I became interested in rocket cars and financed several. Here my idea was born. There was nothing original about it except that I intended to carry it to a definite conclusion. I would travel by rocket to another planet.

"My studies had convinced me that of all the planets Mars alone offered presumptive evidence of habitability for creatures similar to ourselves. I was at the same time convinced that if I succeeded in reaching Mars the probability of my being able to return to earth was remote. Feeling that I must have some reason for embarking upon such a venture, other than selfishness, I determined to seek out some one with whom I could communicate in the event that I succeeded. Subsequently it occurred to me that this might also afford the means for launching a second expedition, equipped to make the return journey, for I had no doubt but that there would be many adventurous spirits ready to undertake such an excursion once I had proved it feasible.

"For over a year I have been engaged in the construction of a gigantic rocket on Guadalupe Island, off the west coast of Lower California. The Mexican government has given me every assistance, and today everything is complete to the last detail. I am ready to start at any moment."

As he ceased speaking, he suddenly faded from view. The chair in which he had been sitting was empty. There was no one in the room but myself. I was stunned, almost terrified. I recalled what Rothmund had said about the effect of the narcotics upon my mentality. I also recalled that insane people seldom realize that they are insane. Was *I* insane! Cold sweat broke out upon my forehead and the backs of my hands. I reached toward the buzzer to summon Ralph. There is no question but that Ralph is sane. If he had seen Carson Napier and shown him into my study—what a relief that would be!

But before my finger touched the button Ralph entered the room. There was a puzzled expression on his face. "Mr. Napier is back again," he said, and then he added, "I didn't know he had left. I just heard him talking to you."

I breathed a sigh of relief as I wiped the perspiration from my face and hands; if I was crazy, so was Ralph. "Bring him in," I said, "and this time you stay here."

When Napier entered there was a questioning look in his eyes. "Do you fully grasp the situation as far as I have explained it?" he asked, as though he had not been out of the room at all.

"Yes, but—" I started.

"Wait, please," he requested. "I know what you are going to say, but let me apologize first and explain. I have not been here before. That was my final test. If you are confident that you saw me and talked to me and can recall what I said to you as I sat outside in my car, then you and I can communicate just as freely and easily when I am on Mars."

"But," interjected Rothmund, "you *were* here. Didn't I shake hands with you when you came in, and talk to you?"

"You thought you did," replied Napier.

"Who's loony now?" I inquired inelegantly, but to this day Rothmund insists that we played a trick on him.

"How do you know he's here now, then?" he asked.

"I don't," I admitted.

"I am, this time," laughed Napier. "Let's see; how far had I gotten?"

"You were saying that you were all ready to start, had your rocket set up on Gaudalupe Island," I reminded him.

"Right! I see you got it all. Now, as briefly as possible, I'll outline what I hope you will find it possible to do for me. I have come to you for several reasons, the more important of which are your interest in Mars, your profession (the results of my experiment must be recorded by an experienced writer), and your reputation for integrity—I have taken the liberty of investigating you most thoroughly. I wish you to record and publish the messages you receive from me and to administer my estate during my absence."

"I shall be glad to do the former, but I hesitate to accept the responsibility of the latter assignment," I demurred.

"I have already arranged a trust that will give you ample protection," he replied in a manner that precluded further argument. I saw that he was a young man who brooked no obstacles; in fact I think he never admitted the existence of an obstacle. "As for your remuneration," he continued, "you may name your own figure."

I waved a deprecatory hand. "It will be a pleasure," I assured him.

"It may take a great deal of your time," interjected Ralph, "and your time is valuable."

"Precisely," agreed Napier. "Mr. Rothmund and I will, with your permission, arrange the financial details later."

"That suits me perfectly," I said, for I detest business and everything connected with it.

"Now, to get back to the more important and far more interesting phases of our discussion; what is your reaction to the plan as a whole?"

"Mars is a long way from earth," I suggested; "Venus is nine or ten million miles closer, and a million miles are a million miles."

"Yes, and I would prefer going to Venus," he replied. "Enveloped in clouds, its surface forever invisible to man, it presents a mystery that intrigues the imagination; but recent astronomical research suggests conditions there inimical to the support of any such life as we know on earth. It has been thought by some that, held in the grip of the Sun since the era of her pristine fluidity, she always presents the same face to him, as does the Moon to earth. If such is the case, the extreme heat of one hemisphere and the extreme cold of the other would preclude life.

"Even if the suggestion of Sir James Jeans is borne out by fact, each of her days and nights is several times as long as ours on earth, these long nights having a temperature of thirteen degrees below zero, Fahrenheit, and the long days a correspondingly high temperature."

"Yet even so, life might have adapted itself to such conditions," I contended; "man exists in equatorial heat and arctic cold."

"But not without oxygen," said Napier. "St. John has estimated that the amount of oxygen above the cloud envelope that surrounds Venus is less than one tenth of one per cent of the terrestrial amount. After all, we have to bow to the superior judgment of such men as Sir James Jeans, who says, 'The evidence, for what it is worth, goes to suggest that Venus, the only planet in the solar system outside Mars and the earth on which life could possibly exist, possesses no vegetation and no oxygen for higher forms of life to breathe,' which definitely limits my planetary exploration to Mars."

We discussed his plans during the remainder of the day and well into the night, and early the following morning he left for Guadalupe Island in his Sikorsky amphibian. I have not seen him since, at least in person, yet, through the marvellous medium of telepathy, I have communicated with him continually and seen him amid strange, unearthly surroundings that have been graphically photographed upon the retina of my mind's eye. Thus I am the medium through which the remarkable adventures of Carson Napier are being recorded on earth; but I am only that, like a typewriter or a dictaphone—the story that follows is his.

CHAPTER TWO

Off for Mars

As I set my ship down in the sheltered cove along the shore of desolate Gaudalupe a trifle over four hours after I left Tarzana, the little Mexican steamer I had chartered to transport my men, materials, and supplies from the mainland rode peacefully at anchor in the tiny harbor, while on the shore, waiting to welcome me, were grouped the laborers, mechanics, and assistants who had worked with such wholehearted loyalty for long months in preparation for this day. Towering head and shoulders above the others loomed Jimmy Welsh, the only American among them.

I taxied in close to shore and moored the ship to a buoy, while the men launched a dory and rowed out to get me. I had been absent less than a week, most of which had been spent in Guaymas awaiting the expected letter from Tarzana, but so exuberantly did they greet me, one might have thought me a long-lost brother returned from the dead, so dreary and desolate and isolated is Guadalupe to those who must remain upon her lonely shores for even a brief interval between contacts with the mainland.

Perhaps the warmth of their greeting may have been enhanced by a desire to conceal their true feelings. We had been together constantly for months, warm friendships had sprung up between us, and tonight we were to separate with little likelihood that they and I should ever meet again. This was to be my last day on earth; after today I should be as dead to them as though three feet of earth covered my inanimate corpse.

It is possible that my own sentiments colored my interpretation of theirs, for I am frank to confess that I had been apprehending this last moment as the most difficult of the whole adventure. I have come in contact with the peoples of many countries, but I recall none with more lovable qualities than Mexicans who have not been contaminated by too close contact with the intolerance and commercialism of Americans. And then there was Jimmy Welsh! It was going to be like parting with a brother when I said good-bye to him. For months he had been begging to go with me; and I knew that he would continue to beg up to the last minute, but I could not risk a single life unnecessarily.

We all piled into the trucks that we had used to transport supplies and materials from the shore to the camp, which lay inland a few miles, and bumped over our makeshift road to the little table-land where the giant torpedo lay upon its mile long track.

"Everything is ready," said Jimmy. "We polished off the last details this morning. Every roller on the track has been inspected by at least a dozen men, we towed the old crate back and forth over the full length of the track three times with the truck, and then repacked all the rollers with grease. Three of us have checked over every item of equipment and supplies individually; we've done about everything but fire the rockets; and now we're ready to go—you *are* going to take me along, aren't you, Car?"

I shook my head. "Please don't, Jimmy," I begged; "I have a perfect right to gamble with my own life, but not with yours; so forget it. But I am going to do something for you," I added, "just as a token of my appreciation of the help you've given me and all that sort of rot. I'm going to give you my ship to remember me by."

He was grateful, of course, but still he could not hide his disappointment in not being allowed to accompany me, which was evidenced by an invidious comparison he drew between the ceiling of the Sikorsky and that of the old crate, as he had affectionately dubbed the great torpedolike rocket that was to bear me out into space in a few hours.

"A thirty-five million mile ceiling," he mourned dolefully; "think of it! Mars for a ceiling!"

"And may I hit the ceiling!" I exclaimed, fervently.

The laying of the track upon which the torpedo was to take off had been the subject of a year of calculation and consultation. The day of departure had been planned far ahead and the exact point at which Mars would rise above the eastern horizon on that night calculated, as well as the time; then it was necessary to make allowances for the rotation of the earth and the attraction of the nearer heavenly bodies. The track was then laid in accordance with these calculations. It was constructed with a very slight drop in the first three quarters of a mile and then rose gradually at an angle of two and one half degrees from horizontal.

A speed of four and one half miles per second at the take-off would be sufficient to neutralize gravity; to overcome it, I must attain a speed of 6.93 miles per second. To allow a sufficient factor of safety I had powered the torpedo to attain a speed of seven miles per second at the end of the runway, which I purposed stepping up to ten miles per second while passing through the earth's atmosphere. What my speed would be through space was problematical, but I based all my calculations on the theory that it would not deviate much from the speed at which I left the earth's atmosphere, until I came within the influence of the gravitational pull of Mars.

The exact instant at which to make the start had also caused me considerable anxiety. I had calculated it again and again, but there were so many factors to be taken into consideration that I had found it expedient to have my figures checked and rechecked by a well-known physicist and an equally prominent astronomer. Their deductions tallied perfectly with mine—the torpedo must start upon its journey toward Mars some time before the red planet rose above the eastern horizon. The trajectory would be along a constantly flattening arc, influenced considerably at first by the earth's gravitational pull, which would decrease inversely as the square of the distance attained. As the torpedo left the earth's surface on a curved tangent, its departure must be so nicely timed that when it eventually escaped the pull of the earth its nose would be directed toward Mars.

On paper, these figures appeared most convincing; but, as the moment approached for my departure, I must confess to a sudden realization that they were based wholly upon theory, and I was struck with the utter folly of my mad venture.

For a moment I was aghast. The enormous torpedo, with its sixty tons, lying there at the end of its mile long track, loomed above me, the semblance of a gargantuan coffin—my coffin, in which I was presently to be dashed to earth, or to the bottom of the Pacific, or cast out into space to wander there to the end of time. I was afraid. I admit it, but it was not so much the fear of death as the effect of the sudden realization of the stupendousness of the cosmic forces against which I had pitted my puny powers that temporarily unnerved me.

Then Jimmy spoke to me. "Let's have a last look at things inside the old crate before you shove off," he suggested, and my nervousness and my apprehensions vanished beneath the spell of his quiet tones and his matter-of-fact manner. I was myself again.

Together we inspected the cabin, where are located the controls, a wide and comfortable berth, a table, a chair, writing materials, and a well-stocked bookshelf. Behind the cabin is a small galley and just behind the galley a storeroom containing canned and dehydrated foods sufficient to last me a year. Back of this is a small battery room containing storage batteries for lighting, heating, and cooking, a dynamo, and a gas engine. The extreme stern compartment is filled with rockets and the intricate mechanical device by which they are fed to the firing chambers by means of the controls in the cabin. Forward of the main cabin is a large compartment in which are located the water and oxygen tanks, as well as a quantity of odds and ends necessary either to my safety or comfort.

Everything, it is needless to say, is fastened securely against the sudden and terrific stress that must accompany the take-off. Once out in space, I anticipate no sense of motion, but the start is going to be rather jarring. To absorb, as much as possible, the shock of the take-off, the rocket consists of two torpedoes, a smaller torpedo within a larger one, the former considerably shorter than the latter and consisting of several sections, each one comprising one of the compartments I have described. Between the inner and outer shells and between each two compartments is installed a system of ingenious hydraulic shock absorbers designed to more or less gradually overcome the inertia of the inner torpedo during the take-off. I trust that it functions properly.

In addition to these precautions against disaster at the start, the chair in which I shall sit before the controls is not only heavily overstuffed but is secured to a track or framework that is equipped with shock absorbers. Furthermore, there are means whereby I may strap myself securely into the chair before taking off.

I have neglected nothing essential to my safety, upon which depends the success of my project.

Following our final inspection of the interior, Jimmy and I clambered to the top of the torpedo for a last inspection of the parachutes, which I hope will sufficiently retard the speed of the rocket after it enters the atmosphere of Mars to permit me to bail out with my own parachute in time to make a safe landing. The main parachutes are in a series of compartments running the full length of the top of the torpedo. To explain them more clearly, I may say that they are a continuous series of batteries of parachutes, each battery consisting of a number of parachutes of increasing diameter from the uppermost, which is the smallest. Each battery is in an individual compartment, and each compartment is covered by a separate hatch that can be opened at the will of the operator by controls in the cabin. Each parachute is anchored to the torpedo by a separate cable. I expect about one half of them to be torn loose while checking the speed of the torpedo sufficiently to permit the others to hold and further retard it to a point where I may safely open the doors and jump with my own parachute and oxygen tank.

The moment for departure was approaching. Jimmy and I had descended to the ground and the most difficult ordeal now faced me—that of saying good-bye to these loyal friends and co-workers. We did not say much, we were too filled with emotion, and there was not a dry eye among us. Without exception none of the Mexican laborers could understand why the nose of the torpedo was not pointed straight up in the air if my intended destination were *Marte.* Nothing could convince them that I would not shoot out a short distance and make a graceful nose dive into the Pacific—that is, if I started at all, which many of them doubted.

There was a handclasp all around, and then I mounted the ladder leaning against the side of the torpedo and entered it. As I closed the door of the outer shell, I saw my friends piling into the trucks and pulling away, for I had given orders that no one should be within a mile of the rocket when I took off, fearing, as I did, the effect upon them of the terrific explosions that must accompany the take-off. Securing the outer door with its great vaultlike bolts, I closed the inner door and fastened it; then I took my seat before the controls and buckled the straps that held me to the chair.

I glanced at my watch. It lacked nine minutes of the zero hour. In nine minutes I should be on my way out into the great void, or in nine minutes I should be dead. If all did not go well, the disaster would follow within a fraction of a split second after I touched the first firing control.

Seven minutes! My throat felt dry and parched; I wanted a drink of water, but there was no time.

Four minutes! Thirty-five million miles are a lot of miles, yet I planned on spanning them in between forty and forty-five days.

Two minutes! I inspected the oxygen gauge and opened the valve a trifle wider.

One minute! I thought of my mother and wondered if she were way out there somewhere waiting for me.

Thirty seconds! My hand was on the control. Fifteen seconds! Ten, five, four, three, two—one!

I turned the pointer! There was a muffled roar. The torpedo leaped forward. I was off!

I knew that the take-off was a success. I glanced through the port at my side at the instant that the torpedo started, but so terrific was its initial speed that I saw only a confused blur as the landscape rushed past. I was thrilled and delighted by the ease and perfection with which the take-off had been accomplished, and I must admit that I was not a little surprised by the almost negligible effects that were noticeable in the cabin. I had had the sensation as of a giant hand pressing me suddenly back against the upholstery of my chair, but that had passed almost at once, and now there was no sensation different from that which one might experience sitting in an easy chair in a comfortable drawing-room on terra firma.

There was no sensation of motion after the first few seconds that were required to pass through the earth's atmosphere, and now that I had done all that lay within my power to do, I could only leave the rest to momentum, gravitation, and fate. Releasing the straps that held me to the chair, I moved about the cabin to look through the various ports, of which there were several in the sides, keel, and top of the torpedo. Space was a black void dotted with countless points of light. The earth I could not see, for it lay directly astern; far ahead was Mars. All seemed well. I switched on the electric lights, and seating myself at the table, made the first entries in the log; then I checked over various computations of time and distances.

My calculations suggested that in about three hours from the take-off the torpedo would be moving almost directly toward Mars; and from time to time I took observations through the wide-angle telescopic periscope that is mounted flush with the upper surface of the torpedo's shell, but the results were not entirely reassuring. In two hours Mars was dead ahead—the arc of the trajectory was not flattening as it should. I became apprehensive. What was wrong? Where had our careful computations erred?

I left the periscope and gazed down through the main keel port. Below and ahead was the Moon, a gorgeous spectacle as viewed through the clear void of space from a distance some seventy-two thousand miles less than I had ever seen it before and with no earthly atmosphere to reduce visibility. Tycho, Plato, and Copernicus stood out in bold relief upon the brazen disc of the great satellite, deepening by contrast the shadows of Mare Serenitatis and Mare Tranquilitatis. The rugged peaks of the Apennine and the Altai lay revealed as distinctly as I had ever seen them through the largest telescope. I was thrilled, but I was distinctly worried, too.

Three hours later I was less than fifty-nine thousand miles from the Moon; where its aspect had been gorgeous before, it now beggared description, but my apprehension had cause to increase in proportion; I might say, as the square of its increasing gorgeousness. Through the periscope I had watched the arc of my trajectory pass through the plane of Mars and drop below it. I knew quite definitely then that I could never reach my goal. I tried not to think of the fate that lay ahead of me; but, instead, sought to discover the error that had wrought this disaster.

For an hour I checked over various calculations, but could discover nothing that might shed light on the cause of my predicament; then I switched off the lights and looked down through the keel port to have a closer view of the Moon. It was not there! Stepping to the port side of the cabin, I looked through one of the heavy circular glasses out into the void of space. For an instant I was horror stricken; apparently just off the port bow loomed an enormous world. It was the Moon, less than twenty-three thousand miles away, and I was hurtling toward it at the rate of thirty-six thousand miles an hour!

I leaped to the periscope, and in the next few seconds I accomplished some lightning mental calculating that must constitute an all-time record. I watched the deflection of our course in the direction of the Moon, following it across the lens of the periscope, I computed the distance to the Moon and the speed of the torpedo, and I came to the conclusion that I had better than a fighting chance of missing the great orb. I had little fear of anything but a direct hit, since our speed was so great that the attraction of the Moon could not hold us if we missed her even by a matter of feet; but it was quite evident that it had affected our flight, and with this realization came the answer to the question that had been puzzling me.

To my mind flashed the printer's story of the first perfect book. It had been said that no book had ever before been published containing not a single error. A great publishing house undertook to publish such a book. The galley proofs were read and reread by a dozen different experts, the page proofs received the same careful scrutiny. At last the masterpiece was ready for the press—errorless! It was printed and bound and sent out to the public, and then it was discovered that the title had been misspelled on the title page. With all our careful calculation, with all our checking and rechecking, we had overlooked the obvious; we had not taken the Moon into consideration at all.

Explain it if you can; I cannot. It was just one of those things, as people say when a good team loses to a poor one; it was a *break,* and a bad one. How bad it was I did not even try to conjecture at the time; I just sat at the periscope watching the Moon racing toward us. As we neared it, it presented the most gorgeous spectacle that I have ever witnessed. Each mountain peak and crater stood out in vivid detail. Even the great height of summits over twenty-five thousand feet appeared distinguishable to me, though imagination must have played a major part in the illusion, since I was looking down upon them from above.

Suddenly I realized that the great sphere was passing rapidly from the field of the periscope, and I breathed a sigh of relief—we were not going to score a clean hit, we were going to pass by.

I returned then to the porthole. The Moon lay just ahead and a little to the left. It was no longer a great sphere; it was a world that filled my whole range of vision. Against its black horizon I saw titanic peaks; below me huge craters yawned. I stood with God on high and looked down upon a dead world.

Our transit of the Moon required a little less than four minutes; I timed it carefully that I might check our speed. How close we came I may only guess; perhaps five thousand feet above the tallest peaks, but it was close enough. The pull of the Moon's gravitation had definitely altered our course, but owing to our speed we had eluded her clutches. Now we were racing away from her, but to what?

The nearest star, Alpha Centauri, is twenty-five and a half million million miles from earth. Write that on your typewriter—25,500,000,000,000 miles. But why trifle with short distances like this? There was little likelihood that I should visit Alpha Centauri with all the wide range of space at my command and many more interesting places to go. I knew that I had ample room in which to wander, since science has calculated the diameter of space to be eighty-four thousand million light years, which, when one reflects that light travels at the rate of one hundred eighty-six thousand miles a second, should satisfy the wanderlust of the most inveterate roamer.

However, I was not greatly concerned with any of these distances, as I had food and water for only a year, during which time the torpedo might travel slightly more than three hundred fifteen million miles. Even if it reached our near neighbor, Alpha Centauri, I should not then be greatly interested in the event, as I should have been dead for over eighty thousand years. Such is the immensity of the universe!

During the next twenty-four hours the course of the torpedo nearly paralleled the Moon's orbit around the earth. Not only had the pull of the Moon deflected its course, but now it seemed evident that the earth had seized us and that we were doomed to race through eternity around her, a tiny, second satellite. But I did not wish to be a moon, certainly not an insignificant moon that in all probability might not be picked up by even the largest telescope.

The next month was the most trying of my life. It seems the height of egotism even to mention my life in the face of the stupendous cosmic forces that engulfed it; but it was the only life I had and I was fond of it, and the more imminent seemed the moment when it should be snuffed out, the better I liked it.

At the end of the second day it was quite apparent that we had eluded the grip of the earth. I cannot say that I was elated at the discovery. My plan to visit Mars was ruined. I should have been glad to return to earth. If I could have landed safely on Mars, I certainly could have landed safely on earth. But there was another reason why I should have been glad to have returned to earth, a reason that loomed, large and terrible, ahead—the Sun. We were heading straight for the Sun now. Once in the grip of that mighty power, nothing could affect our destiny; we were doomed. For three months I must await the inevitable end, before plunging into that fiery furnace. Furnace is an inadequate word by which to suggest the Sun's heat, which is reputedly from thirty to sixty million degrees at the center, a fact which should not have concerned me greatly, since I did not anticipate reaching the center.

The days dragged on, or, I should say, the long night—there were no days, other than the record that I kept of the passing hours. I read a great deal. I made no entries in the log. Why write something that was presently to be plunged into the Sun and consumed? I experimented in the galley, attempting fancy cooking. I ate a great deal; it helped to pass the time away, and I enjoyed my meals.

On the thirtieth day I was scanning space ahead when I saw a gorgeous, shimmering crescent far to the right of our course; but I must confess that I was not greatly interested in sights of any sort. In sixty days I should be in the Sun. Long before that, however, the increasing heat would have destroyed me. The end was approaching rapidly.

CHAPTER THREE

Rushing toward Venus

The psychological effects of an experience such as that through which I had been passing must be considerable, and even though they could be neither weighed nor measured, I was yet conscious of changes that had taken place in me because of them. For thirty days I had been racing alone through space toward absolute annihilation, toward an end that would probably not leave a single nucleus of the atoms that compose me an electron to carry on with, I had experienced the ultimate in solitude, and the result had been to deaden my sensibilities; doubtless a wise provision of nature.

Even the realization that the splendid crescent, looming enormously off the starboard bow of the torpedo, was Venus failed to excite me greatly. What if I were to approach Venus more closely than any other human being of all time! It meant nothing. Were I to see God, himself, even that would mean nothing. It became apparent that the value of what we see is measurable only by the size of our prospective audience. Whatever I saw, who might never have an audience, was without value.

Nevertheless, more to pass away the time than because I was particularly interested in the subject, I began to make some rough calculations. These indicated that I was about eight hundred sixty-five thousand miles from the orbit of Venus and that I should cross it in about twenty-four hours. I could not, however, compute my present distance from the planet accurately. I only knew that it appeared very close. When I say close, I mean relatively. The earth was some twenty-five million miles away, the Sun about sixty-eight million, so that an object as large as Venus, at a distance of one or two million miles, appeared close.

As Venus travels in her orbit at the rate of nearly twenty-two miles per second, or over one million six hundred thousand miles in a terrestrial day, it appeared evident to me that she would cross my path some time within the next twenty-four hours.

It occurred to me that, passing closely, as was unavoidable, she might deflect the course of the torpedo and save me from the Sun; but I knew this to be a vain hope. Undoubtedly, the path of the torpedo would be bent, but the Sun would not relinquish his prey. With these thoughts, my apathy returned, and I lost interest in Venus.

Selecting a book, I lay down on my bed to read. The interior of the cabin was brightly illuminated. I am extravagant with electricity. I have the means of generating it for eleven more months; but I shall not need it after a few weeks, so why should I be parsimonious?

I read for a few hours, but as reading in bed always makes me sleepy, I eventually succumbed. When I awoke, I lay for a few minutes in luxurious ease. I might be racing toward extinction at the rate of thirty-six thousand miles an hour, but I, myself, was unhurried. I recalled the beautiful spectacle that Venus had presented when I had last observed her and decided to have another look at her. Stretching languorously, I arose and stepped to one of the starboard portholes.

The picture framed by the casing of that circular opening was gorgeous beyond description. Apparently less than half as far away as before, and twice as large, loomed the mass of Venus outlined by an aureole of light where the Sun, behind her, illuminated her cloudy envelope and lighted to burning brilliance a thin crescent along the edge nearest me.

I looked at my watch. Twelve hours had passed since I first discovered the planet, and now, at last, I became excited. Venus was apparently half as far away as it had been twelve hours ago, and I knew that the torpedo had covered half the distance that had separated us from her orbit at that time. A collision was possible, it even seemed within the range of probability that I should be dashed to the surface of this inhospitable, lifeless world.

Well, what of it? Am I not already doomed? What difference can it make to me if the end comes a few weeks sooner than I had anticipated? Yet I was excited. I cannot say that I felt fear. I have no fear of death—that left me when my mother died; but now that the great adventure loomed so close I was overwhelmed by contemplation of it and the great wonder that it induced. What would follow?

The long hours dragged on. It seemed incredible to me, accustomed though I am to thinking in units of terrific speed, that the torpedo and Venus were racing toward the same point in her orbit at such inconceivable velocities, the one at the rate of thirty-six thousand miles per hour, the other at over sixty-seven thousand.

It was now becoming difficult to view the planet through the side port, as she moved steadily closer and closer to our path. I went to the periscope—she was gliding majestically within its range. I knew that at that moment the torpedo was less than thirty-six thousand miles, less than an hour, from the path of the planet's orbit, and there could be no doubt now but that she had already seized us in her grasp. We were destined to make a clean hit. Even under the circumstances I could not restrain a smile at the thought of the marksmanship that this fact revealed. I had aimed at Mars and was about to hit Venus; unquestionably the all-time cosmic record for poor shots.

Even though I did not shrink from death, even though the world's best astronomers have assured us that Venus must be unfitted to support human life, that where her surface is not unutterably hot it is unutterably cold, even though she be oxygenless, as they aver, yet the urge to live that is born with each of us compelled me to make the same preparations to land that I should have had I successfully reached my original goal, Mars.

Slipping into a fleece-lined suit of coveralls, I donned goggles and a fleece-lined helmet; then I adjusted the oxygen tank that was designed to hang in front of me, lest it foul the parachute, and which can be automatically jettisoned in the event that I reach an atmosphere that will support life, for it would be an awkward and dangerous appendage to be cumbered with while landing. Finally, I adjusted my chute.

I glanced at my watch. If my calculations have been correct, we should strike in about fifteen minutes. Once more I returned to the periscope.

The sight that met my eyes was awe inspiring. We were plunging toward a billowing mass of black clouds. It was like chaos on the dawn of creation. The gravitation of the planet had seized us. The floor of the cabin was no longer beneath me—I was standing on the forward bulkhead now; but this condition I had anticipated when I designed the torpedo. We were diving nose on toward the planet. In space there had been neither up nor down, but now there was a very definite down.

From where I stood I could reach the controls, and beside me was the door in the side of the torpedo. I released three batteries of parachutes and opened the door in the wall of the inner torpedo. There was a noticeable jar, as though the parachutes had opened and temporarily checked the speed of the torpedo. This must mean that I had entered an atmosphere of some description and that there was not a second to waste.

With a single movement of a lever I loosed the remaining parachutes; then I turned to the outer door. Its bolts were controlled by a large wheel set in the center of the door and were geared to open quickly and with ease. I adjusted the mouthpiece of the oxygen line across my lips and quickly spun the wheel.

Simultaneously the door flew open and the air pressure within the torpedo shot me out into space. My right hand grasped the rip cord of my chute; but I waited. I looked about for the torpedo. It was racing almost parallel with me, all its parachutes distended above it. Just an instant's glimpse I had of it, and then it dove into the cloud mass and was lost to view; but what a weirdly magnificent spectacle it had presented in that brief instant!

Safe now from any danger of fouling with the torpedo, I jerked the rip cord of my parachute just as the clouds swallowed me. Through my fleece-lined suit I felt the bitter cold; like a dash of ice water the cold clouds slapped me in the face; then, to my relief, the chute opened, and I fell more slowly.

Down, down, down I dropped. I could not even guess the duration, nor the distance. It was very dark and very wet, like sinking into the depths of the ocean without feeling the pressure of the water. My thoughts during those long moments were such as to baffle description. Perhaps the oxygen made me a little drunk; I do not know. I felt exhilarated and intensely eager to solve the great mystery beneath me. The thought that I was about to die did not concern me so much as what I might see before I died. I was about to land on Venus—the first human being in all the world to see the face of the veiled planet.

Suddenly I emerged into a cloudless space; but far below me were what appeared in the darkness to be more clouds, recalling to my mind the often advanced theory of the two cloud envelopes of Venus. As I descended, the temperature rose gradually, but it was still cold.

As I entered the second cloud bank, there was a very noticeable rise in temperature the farther I fell. I shut off the oxygen supply and tried breathing through my nose. By inhaling deeply I discovered that I could take in sufficient oxygen to support life, and an astronomical theory was shattered. Hope flared within me like a beacon on a fog-hid landing field.

As I floated gently downward, I presently became aware of a faint luminosity far below. What could it be? There were many obvious reasons why it could not be sunlight; sunlight would not come from below, and, furthermore, it was night on this hemisphere of the planet. Naturally many weird conjectures raced through my mind. I wondered if this could be the light from an incandescent world, but immediately discarded that explanation as erroneous, knowing that the heat from an incandescent world would long since have consumed me. Then it occurred to me that it might be refracted light from that portion of the cloud envelope illuminated by the Sun, yet if such were the case, it seemed obvious that the clouds about me should be luminous, which they were not.

There seemed only one practical solution. It was the solution that an earth man would naturally arrive at. Being what I am, a highly civilized creature from a world already far advanced by science and invention, I attributed the source of this light to these twin forces of superior intelligence. I could only account for that faint glow by attributing it to the reflection upon the under side of the cloud mass of artificial light produced by intelligent creatures upon the surface of this world toward which I was slowly settling.

I wondered what these beings would be like, and if my excitement grew as I anticipated the wonders that were soon to be revealed to my eyes, I believe that it was a pardonable excitement, under the circumstances. Upon the threshold of such an adventure who would not have been moved to excitement by contemplation of the experiences awaiting him?

Now I removed the mouthpiece of the oxygen tube entirely and found that I could breathe easily. The light beneath me was increasing gradually. About me I thought I saw vague, dark shapes among the cloud masses. Shadows, perhaps, but of what? I detached the oxygen tank and let it fall. I distinctly heard it strike something an instant after I had released it. Then a shadow loomed darkly beneath me, and an instant later my feet struck something that gave beneath them.

I dropped into a mass of foliage and grasped wildly for support. A moment later I began to fall more rapidly and guessed what had happened; the parachute had been uptilted by contact with the foliage. I clutched at leaves and branches, fruitlessly, and then I was brought to a sudden stop; evidently the chute had fouled something. I hoped that it would hold until I found a secure resting place.

As I groped about in the dark, my hand finally located a sturdy branch, and a moment later I was astride it, my back to the bole of a large tree—another theory gone the ignoble path of countless predecessors; it was evident that there was vegetation on Venus. At least there was one tree; I could vouch for that, as I was sitting in it, and doubtless the black shadows I had passed were other, taller trees.

Having found secure lodgment, I divested myself of my parachute after salvaging some of its ropes and the straps from the harness, which I thought I might find helpful in descending the tree. Starting at the top of a tree, in darkness and among clouds, one may not be positive what the tree is like nearer the ground. I also removed my goggles. Then I commenced to descend. The girth of the tree was enormous, but the branches grew sufficiently close together to permit me to find safe footing.

I did not know how far I had fallen through the second cloud stratum before I lodged in the tree nor how far I had descended the tree, but all together it must have been close to two thousand feet; yet I was still in the clouds. Could the entire atmosphere of Venus be forever fog laden? I hoped not, for it was a dreary prospect.

The light from below had increased a little as I descended, but not much; it was still dark about me. I continued to descend. It was tiresome work and not without danger, this climbing down an unfamiliar tree in a fog, at night, toward an unknown world. But I could not remain where I was, and there was nothing above to entice me upward; so I continued to descend.

What a strange trick fate had played me. I had wanted to visit Venus, but had discarded the idea when assured by my astronomer friends that the planet could not support either animal or vegetable life. I had started for Mars, and now, fully ten days before I had hoped to reach the red planet, I was on Venus, breathing perfectly good air among the branches of a tree that evidently dwarfed the giant Sequoias.

The illumination was increasing rapidly now, the clouds were thinning; through breaks I caught glimpses far below, glimpses of what appeared to be an endless vista of foliage, softly moonlit—but Venus had no moon. In that, insofar as the seeming moonlight was concerned, I could fully concur with the astronomers. This illumination came from no moon, unless Venus's satellite lay beneath her inner envelope of clouds, which was preposterous.

A moment later I emerged entirely from the cloud bank, but though I searched in all directions, I saw nothing but foliage, above, around, below me, yet I could see far down into that abyss of leaves. In the soft light I could not determine the color of the foliage, but I was sure that it was not green; it was some light, delicate shade of another color.

I had descended another thousand feet since I had emerged from the clouds, and I was pretty well exhausted (the month of inactivity and overeating had softened me), when I saw just below me what appeared to be a causeway leading from the tree I was descending to another adjacent. I also discovered that from just below where I clung the limbs had been cut away from the tree to a point below the causeway. Here were two startling and unequivocal evidences of the presence of intelligent beings. Venus was inhabited! But by what? What strange, arboreal creatures built causeways high among these giant trees? Were they a species of monkey-man? Were they of a high or low order of intelligence? How would they receive me?

At this juncture in my vain speculations I was startled by a noise above me. Something was moving in the branches overhead. The sound was coming nearer, and it seemed to me that it was being made by something of considerable size and weight, but perhaps, I realized, that conjecture was the child of my imagination. However, I felt most uncomfortable. I was unarmed. I have never carried weapons. My friends had urged a perfect arsenal upon me before I embarked upon my adventure, but I had argued that if I arrived on Mars unarmed it would be *prima facie* evidence of my friendly intentions, and even if my reception were warlike, I should be no worse off, since I could not hope, single-handed, to conquer a world, no matter how well armed I were.

Suddenly, above me, to the crashing of some heavy body through the foliage were added hideous screams and snarls; and in the terrifying dissonance I recognized the presence of more than a single creature. Was I being pursued by all the fearsome denizens of this Venusan forest!

Perhaps my nerves were slightly unstrung; and who may blame them if they were, after what I had passed through so recently and during the long, preceding month? They were not entirely shattered, however, and I could still appreciate the fact that night noises often multiply themselves in a most disconcerting way. I have heard coyotes yapping and screaming around my camp on Arizona nights when, but for the actual knowledge that there were but one or two of them, I could have sworn that there were a hundred, had I trusted only to my sense of hearing.

But in this instance I was quite positive that the voices of more than a single beast were mingling to produce the horrid din that, together with the sound of their passage, was definitely and unquestionably drawing rapidly nearer me. Of course I did not know that the owners of those awesome voices were pursuing me, though a still, small voice within seemed to be assuring me that such was the fact.

I wished that I might reach the causeway below me (I should feel better standing squarely on two feet), but it was too far to drop and there were no more friendly branches to give me support; then I thought of the ropes I had salvaged from the abandoned parachute. Quickly uncoiling them from about my waist, I looped one of them over the branch upon which I sat, grasped both strands firmly in my hands, and prepared to swing from my porch. Suddenly the screams and snarling growls ceased; and then, close above me now, I heard the noise of something descending toward me and saw the branches shaking to its weight.

Lowering my body from the branch, I swung downward and slid the fifteen or more feet to the causeway, and as I alighted the silence of the great forest was again shattered by a hideous scream just above my head. Looking up quickly, I saw a creature launching itself toward me and just beyond it a snarling face of utter hideousness. I caught but the briefest glimpse of it—just enough to see that it was a face, with eyes and a mouth—then it was withdrawn amidst the foliage.

Perhaps I only sensed that hideous vision subconsciously at the time, for the whole scene was but a flash upon the retina of my eye, and the other beast was in mid-air above me at the instant; but it remained indelibly impressed upon my memory, and I was to recall it upon a later day under circumstances so harrowing that the mind of mortal earth man may scarce conceive them.

As I leaped back to avoid the creature springing upon me, I still clung to one strand of the rope down which I had lowered myself to the causeway. My grasp upon the rope was unconscious and purely mechanical; it was in my hand, and my fist was clenched; and as I leaped away, I dragged the rope with me. A fortuitous circumstance, no doubt, but a most fortunate one.

The creature missed me, alighting on all fours a few feet from me, and there it crouched, apparently slightly bewildered, and, fortunately for me, it did not immediately charge, giving me the opportunity to collect my wits and back slowly away, at the same time mechanically coiling the rope in my right hand. The little, simple things one does in moments of stress or excitement often seem entirely beyond reason and incapable of explanation; but I have thought that they may be dictated by a subconscious mind reacting to the urge of self-preservation. Possibly they are not always well directed and may as often fail to be of service as not, but then it may be possible that subconscious minds are no less fallible than the objective mind, which is wrong far more often than it is right. I cannot but seek for some explanation of the urge that caused me to retain that rope, since, all unknown to me, it was to be the slender thread upon which my life was to hang.

Silence had again descended upon the weird scene. Since the final scream of the hideous creature that had retreated into the foliage after this thing had leaped for me, there had been no sound. The creature that crouched facing me seemed slightly bewildered. I am positive now that it had not been pursuing me, but that it itself had been the object of pursuit by the other beast that had retreated.

In the dim half-light of the Venusan night I saw confronting me a creature that might be conjured only in the half-delirium of some horrid nightmare. It was about as large as a full-grown puma, and stood upon four handlike feet that suggested that it might be almost wholly arboreal. The front legs were much longer than the hind, suggesting, in this respect, the hyena; but here the similarity ceased, for the creature's furry pelt was striped longitudinally with alternate bands of red and yellow, and its hideous head bore no resemblance to any earthly animal. No external ears were visible, and in the low forehead was a single large, round eye at the end of a thick antenna about four inches long. The jaws were powerful and armed with long, sharp fangs, while from either side of the neck projected a powerful chela. Never have I seen a creature so fearsomely armed for offense as was this nameless beast of another world. With those powerful crablike pincers it could easily have held an opponent far stronger than a man and dragged it to those terrible jaws.

For a time it eyed me with that single, terrifying eye that moved to and fro at the end of its antenna, and all the time its chelæ were waving slowly, opening and closing. In that brief moment of delay I looked about me, and the first thing that I discovered was that I stood directly in front of an opening cut in the bole of the tree; an opening about three feet wide and over six feet high. But the most remarkable thing about it was that it was closed by a door; not a solid door, but one suggesting a massive wooden grill.

As I stood contemplating it and wondering what to do, I thought that I saw something moving behind it. Then a voice spoke to me out of the darkness beyond the door. It sounded like a human voice, though it spoke in a language that I could not understand. The tones were peremptory. I could almost imagine that it said, "Who are you, and what do you want here in the middle of the night?"

"I am a stranger," I said. "I come in peace and friendship."

Of course I knew that whatever it was behind that door, it could not understand me; but I hoped that my tone would assure it of my peaceful designs. There was a moment's silence and then I heard other voices. Evidently the situation was being discussed; then I saw that the creature facing me upon the causeway was creeping toward me, and I turned my attention from the doorway to the beast.

I had no weapons, nothing but a length of futile rope; but I knew that I must do something. I could not stand there supinely and let the creature seize and devour me without striking a blow in my own defense. I uncoiled a portion of the rope and, more in despair than with any hope that I could accomplish anything of a defensive nature, flicked the end of it in the face of the advancing beast. You have seen a boy snap a wet towel at a companion; perhaps you have been flicked in that way, and if you have, you know that it hurts.

Of course I did not expect to overcome my adversary by any such means as this; to be truthful, I did not know what I did expect to accomplish. Perhaps I just felt that I must do something, and this was the only thing that occurred to me. The result merely demonstrated the efficiency of that single eye and the quickness of the chelæ. I snapped that rope as a ringmaster snaps a whip; but though the rope end travelled with great speed and the act must have been unexpected, the creature caught the rope in one of its chelæ before it reached its face. Then it hung on and sought to drag me toward those frightful jaws.

I learned many a trick of roping from a cowboy friend of my motion picture days, and one of these I now put into use in an endeavor to entangle the crablike chelæ. Suddenly giving the rope sufficient slack, I threw a half hitch around the chela that gripped it, immediately following it with a second, whereupon the creature commenced to pull desperately away. I think it was motivated solely by an instinctive urge to pull toward its jaws anything that was held in its chelæ; but for how long it would continue to pull away before it decided to change its tactics and charge me, I could not even guess; and so I acted upon a sudden inspiration and hurriedly made fast the end of the rope that I held to one of the stout posts that supported the handrail of the causeway; then, of a sudden, the thing charged me, roaring furiously.

I turned and ran, hoping that I could get out of the reach of those terrible chelæ before the creature was stopped by the rope; and this I but barely managed to do. I breathed a sigh of relief as I saw the great body flipped completely over on its back as the rope tautened, but the hideous scream of rage that followed left me cold. Nor was my relief of any great duration, for as soon as the creature had scrambled to its feet, it seized the rope in its other chela and severed it as neatly as one might with a pair of monstrous tinner's snips; and then it was after me again, but this time it did not creep.

It seemed evident that my stay upon Venus was to be brief, when suddenly the door in the tree swung open and three men leaped to the causeway just behind the charging terror that was swiftly driving down upon me. The leading man hurled a short, heavy spear that sank deep into the back of my infuriated pursuer. Instantly the creature stopped in its tracks and wheeled about to face these new and more dangerous tormentors; and as he did so two more spears, hurled by the companions of the first man, drove into his chest, and with a last frightful scream, the thing dropped in its tracks, dead.

Then the leading man came toward me. In the subdued light of the forest he appeared no different from an earth man. He held the point of a straight, sharp sword pointed at my vitals. Close behind him were the other two men, each with a drawn sword.

The first man spoke to me in a stern, commanding voice, but I shook my head to indicate that I could not understand; then he pressed the point of his weapon against my coveralls, opposite the pit of my stomach, and jabbed. I backed away. He advanced and jabbed at me again, and again I backed along the causeway. Now the other two men advanced and the three of them fell to examining me, meanwhile talking among themselves.

I could see them better now. They were about my own height and in every detail of their visible anatomy they appeared identical with terrestrial human beings, nor was a great deal left to my imagination—

the men were almost naked. They wore loincloths and little else other than the belts that supported the scabbards of their swords. Their skins appeared to be much darker than mine, but not so dark as a negro's, and their faces were smooth and handsome.

Several times one or another of them addressed me and I always replied, but neither understood what the other said. Finally, after a lengthy discussion, one of them reentered the opening in the tree and a moment later I saw the interior of a chamber, just within the doorway, illuminated; then one of the two remaining men motioned me forward and pointed toward the doorway.

Understanding that he wished me to enter, I stepped forward, and, as I passed them, they kept their sword points against my body—they were taking no chances with me. The other man awaited me in the center of a large room hewn from the interior of the great tree. Beyond him were other doorways leading from this room, doubtless into other apartments. There were chairs and a table in the room; the walls were carved and painted; there was a large rug upon the floor; from a small vessel depending from the center of the ceiling a soft light illuminated the interior as brightly as might sunlight flooding through an open window, but there was no glare.

The other men had entered and closed the door, which they fastened by a device that was not apparent to me at the time; then one of them pointed to a chair and motioned me to be seated. Under the bright light they examined me intently, and I them. My clothing appeared to puzzle them most; they examined and discussed its material, texture, and weave, if I could judge correctly by their gestures and inflections.

Finding the heat unendurable in my fleece-lined coveralls, I removed them and my leather coat and polo shirt. Each newly revealed article aroused their curiosity and comment. My light skin and blond hair also received their speculative attention.

Presently one of them left the chamber, and while he was absent another removed the various articles that had lain upon the table. These consisted of what I took to be books bound in wooden and in leather covers, several ornaments, and a dagger in a beautifully wrought sheath.

When the man who had left the room returned, he brought food and drink which he placed upon the table; and by signs the three indicated that I might eat. There were fruits and nuts in highly polished, carved wooden bowls; there was something I took to be bread, on a golden platter; and there was honey in a silver jug. A tall, slender goblet contained a whitish liquid that resembled milk. This last receptacle was a delicate, translucent ceramic of an exquisite blue shade. These things and the appointments of the room bespoke culture, refinement, and good taste, making the savage apparel of their owners appear incongruous.

The fruits and nuts were unlike any with which I was familiar, both in appearance and flavor; the bread was coarse but delicious; and the honey, if such it were, suggested candied violets to the taste. The milk (I can find no other earthly word to describe it) was strong and almost pungent, yet far from unpleasant. I imagined at the time that one might grow to be quite fond of it.

The table utensils were similar to those with which we are familiar in civilized portions of the earth; there were hollowed instruments with which to dip or scoop, sharp ones with which to cut, and others with tines with which to impale. There was also a handled pusher, which I recommend to earthly hostesses. All these were of metal.

While I ate, the three men conversed earnestly, one or another of them occasionally offering me more food. They seemed hospitable and courteous, and I felt that if they were typical of the inhabitants of Venus I should find my life here a pleasant one. That it would not be a bed of roses, however, was attested by the weapons that the men constantly wore; one does not carry a sword and a dagger about with him unless he expects to have occasion to use them, except on dress parade.

When I had finished my meal, two of the men escorted me from the room by a rear doorway, up a flight of circular stairs, and ushered me into a small chamber. The stairway and corridor were illuminated by a small lamp similar to that which hung in the room where I had eaten, and light from this lamp shone through the heavy wooden grating of the door, into the room where I was now locked and where my captors left me to my own devices.

Upon the floor was a soft mattress over which were spread coverings of a silky texture. It being very warm, I removed all of my clothing except my undershorts and lay down to sleep. I was tired after my arduous descent of the giant tree and dozed almost immediately. I should have been asleep at once had I not been suddenly startled to wakefulness by a repetition of that hideous scream with which the beast that had pursued me through the tree had announced its rage and chagrin when I had eluded it.

However, it was not long before I fell asleep, my dozing mind filled with a chaos of fragmentary recollections of my stupendous adventure.

CHAPTER FOUR

To the House of the King

When I awoke, it was quite light in the room, and through a window I saw the foliage of trees, lavender and heliotrope and violet in the light of a new day. I arose and went to the window. I saw no sign of sunlight, yet a brightness equivalent to sunlight pervaded everything. The air was warm and sultry. Below me I could see sections of various causeways extending from tree to tree. On some of these I caught glimpses of people. All the men were naked, except for loincloths, nor did I wonder at their scant apparel, in the light of my experience of the temperatures on Venus. There were both men and women; and all the men were armed with swords and daggers, while the women carried daggers only. All those whom I saw seemed to be of the same age; there were neither children nor old people among them. All appeared comely.

From my barred window I sought a glimpse of the ground, but as far down as I could see there was only the amazing foliage of the trees, lavender, heliotrope, and violet. And what trees! From my window I could see several enormous boles fully two hundred feet in diameter. I had thought the tree I descended a giant, but compared with these, it was only a sapling.

As I stood contemplating the scene before me, there was a noise at the door behind me. Turning, I saw one of my captors entering the room. He greeted me with a few words, which I could not understand,

and a pleasant smile, that I could. I returned his smile and said, "Good morning!"

He beckoned to me to follow him from the room, but I made signs indicating that I wished to don my clothes first. I knew I should be hot and uncomfortable in them; I was aware that no one I had seen here wore any clothing, yet so powerful are the inhibitions of custom and habit that I shrank from doing the sensible thing and wearing only my undershorts.

At first, when he realized what I wished to do, he motioned me to leave my clothes where they were and come with him as I was; but eventually he gave in with another of his pleasant smiles. He was a man of fine physique, a little shorter than I; by daylight, I could see that his skin was about that shade of brown that a heavy sun tan imparts to people of my own race; his eyes were dark brown, his hair black. His appearance formed a marked contrast to my light skin, blue eyes, and blond hair.

When I had dressed, I followed him downstairs to a room adjoining the one I had first entered the previous night. Here the man's two companions and two women were seated at a table on which were a number of vessels containing food. As I entered the room the women's eyes were turned upon me curiously; the men smiled and greeted me as had their fellow, and one of them motioned me to a chair. The women appraised me frankly but without boldness, and it was evident that they were discussing me freely between themselves and with the men. They were both uncommonly good-looking, their skins being a shade lighter than those of the men, while their eyes and hair were of about the same color as those of their male companions. Each wore a single garment of a silken material similar to that of which my bed had been made and in the form of a long sash, which was wrapped tightly around the body below the armpits, confining the breasts. From this point it was carried half way around the body downward to the waist, where it circled the body again, the loose end then passing between the legs from behind and up through the sash in front, after the manner of a G string, the remainder falling in front to the knees.

In addition to these garments, which were beautifully embroidered in colors, the women wore girdles from which depended pocket pouches and sheathed daggers, and both were plentifully adorned with ornaments such as rings, bracelets, and hair ornaments. I could recognize gold and silver among the various materials of which these things were fabricated, and there were others that might have been ivory and coral; but what impressed me most was the exquisite workmanship they displayed, and I imagined that they were valued more for this than for the intrinsic worth of the materials that composed them. That this conjecture might be in accordance with fact was borne out by the presence among their ornaments of several of the finest workmanship, obviously carved from ordinary bone.

On the table was bread different from that which I had had the night before, a dish that I thought might be eggs and meat baked together, several which I could not recognize either by appearance or taste, and the familiar milk and honey that I had encountered before. The foods varied widely in range of flavor, so that it would have been a difficult palate indeed that would not have found something to its liking.

During the meal they engaged in serious discussion, and I was certain from their glances and gestures that I was the subject of their debate. The two girls enlivened the meal by attempting to carry on a conversation with me, which appeared to afford them a great deal of merriment, nor could I help joining in their laughter, so infectious was it. Finally one of them hit upon the happy idea of teaching me their language. She pointed to herself and said, "Zuro," and to the other girl and said, "Alzo"; then the men became interested, and I soon learned that the name of him who seemed to be the head of the house, the man who had first challenged me the preceding night, was Duran, the other two Olthar and Kamlot.

But before I had mastered more than these few words and the names of some of the foods on the table, breakfast was over and the three men had conducted me from the house. As we proceeded along the causeway that passed in front of the house of Duran, the interest and curiosity of those we passed were instantly challenged as their eyes fell upon me; and it was at once evident to me that I was a type either entirely unknown on Venus or at least rare, for my blue eyes and blond hair caused quite as much comment as my clothing, as I could tell by their gestures and the direction of their gaze.

We were often stopped by curious friends of my captors, or hosts (I was not sure yet in which category they fell); but none offered me either harm or insult, and if I were the object of their curious scrutiny, so were they of mine. While no two of them were identical in appearance, they were all handsome and all apparently of about the same age. I saw no old people and no children.

Presently we approached a tree of such enormous diameter that I could scarcely believe the testimony of my eyes when I saw it. It was fully five hundred feet in diameter. Stripped of branches for a hundred feet above and below the causeway, its surface was dotted with windows and doors and encircled by wide balconies or verandas. Before a large and elaborately carved doorway was a group of armed men before whom we halted while Duran addressed one of their number.

I thought at the time that he called this man Tofar, and such I learned later was his name. He wore a necklace from which depended a metal disc bearing a hieroglyphic in relief; otherwise he was not accoutered differently from his companions. As he and Duran conversed, he appraised me carefully from head to feet. Presently he and Duran passed through the doorway into the interior of the tree, while the others continued to examine me and question Kamlot and Olthar.

While I waited there, I embraced the opportunity to study the elaborate carvings that surrounded the portal, forming a frame fully five feet wide. The *motif* appeared historical, and I could easily imagine that the various scenes depicted important events in the life of a dynasty or a nation. The workmanship was exquisite, and it required no stretch of the imagination to believe that each delicately carved face was the portrait of some dead or living celebrity. There was nothing grotesque in the delineation of the various figures, as is so often the case in work of a similar character on earth, and only the borders that framed the whole and separated contiguous plaques were conventional.

I was still engrossed by these beautiful examples of the wood carver's art when Duran and Tofar returned and motioned Olthar and Kamlot and me to follow them into the interior of the great tree. We passed through several large chambers and along wide corridors, all carved from the wood of the living tree, to the head of a splendid stairway, which we descended to another level. The chambers near the periphery of the tree received their light through windows, while the interior chambers and corridors were illuminated by lamps similar to those I had already seen in the house of Duran.

Near the foot of the stairway we had descended we entered a spacious chamber, before the doorway to which stood two men armed with spears and swords, and before us, across the chamber, we saw a man seated at a table near a large window. Just inside the doorway we halted, my companions standing in respectful silence until the man at the table looked up and spoke to them; then they crossed the room, taking me with them, and halted before the table, upon the opposite side of which the man sat facing us.

He spoke pleasantly to my companions, calling each by name, and when they replied they addressed him as Jong. He was a fine-looking man with a strong face and a commanding presence. His attire was similar to that worn by all the other male Venusans I had seen, differing only in that he wore about his head a fillet that supported a circular metal disc in the center of his forehead. He appeared much interested in me and watched me intently while listening to Duran, who, I had no doubt, was narrating the story of my strange and sudden appearance the night before.

When Duran had concluded, the man called Jong addressed me. His manner was serious, his tones kindly. Out of courtesy, I replied, though I knew that he could understand me no better than I had understood him. He smiled and shook his head; then he fell into a discussion with the others. Finally he struck a metal gong that stood near him on the table; then he arose and came around the table to where I stood. He examined my clothing carefully, feeling its texture and apparently discussing the materials and the weave with the others. Then he examined the skin of my hands and face, felt of my hair, and made me open my mouth that he might examine my teeth. I was reminded of the horse market and the slave block. "Perhaps," I thought, "the latter is more apropos."

A man entered now whom I took to be a servant and, receiving instructions from the man called Jong, departed again, while I continued to be the object of minute investigation. My beard, which was now some twenty-four hours old, elicited considerable comment. It is not a beautiful beard at any age, being sparse and reddish, for which reason I am careful to shave daily when I have the necessary utensils.

I cannot say that I enjoyed this intimate appraisal, but the manner in which it was conducted was so entirely free from any suggestion of intentional rudeness or discourtesy, and my position here was so delicate that my better judgment prevented me from openly resenting the familiarities of the man called Jong. It is well that I did not.

Presently a man entered through a doorway at my right. I assumed that he had been summoned by the servant recently dispatched. As he came forward, I saw that he was much like the others; a handsome man of about thirty. There are those who declaim against monotony; but for me there can never be any monotony of beauty, not even if the beautiful things were all identical, which the Venusans I had so far seen were not. All were beautiful, but each in his own way.

The man called Jong spoke to the newcomer rapidly for about five minutes, evidently narrating all that they knew about me and giving instructions. When he had finished, the other motioned me to follow him; and a few moments later I found myself in another room on the same level. It had three large windows and was furnished with several desks, tables, and chairs. Most of the available wall space was taken up by shelves on which reposed what I could only assume to be books—thousands of them.

The ensuing three weeks were as delightful and interesting as any that I have ever experienced. During this time, Danus, in whose charge I had been placed, taught me the Venusan language and told me much concerning the planet, the people among whom I had fallen, and their history. I found the language easy to master, but I shall not at this time attempt to describe it fully. The alphabet consists of twenty-four characters, five of which represent vowel sounds, and these are the only vowel sounds that the Venusan vocal chords seem able to articulate. The characters of the alphabet all have the same value, there being no capital letters. Their system of punctuation differs from ours and is more practical; for example, before you start to read a sentence you know whether it is exclamatory, interrogative, a reply to an interrogation, or a simple statement. Characters having values similar to the comma and semicolon are used much as we use these two; they have no colon;

their character that functions as does our period follows each sentence, their question mark and exclamation point preceding the sentences the nature of which they determine.

A peculiarity of their language that renders it easy to master is the absence of irregular verbs; the verb root is never altered for voice, mode, tense, number, or person, distinctions that are achieved by the use of several simple, auxiliary words.

While I was learning to speak the language of my hosts, I also learned to read and write it, and I spent many enjoyable hours delving into the large library of which Danus is the curator while my tutor was absent attending to his other duties, which are numerous. He is chief physician and surgeon of his country, physician and surgeon to the king, and head of a college of medicine and surgery.

One of the first questions that Danus had asked me when I had acquired a working knowledge of his language was where I came from, but when I told him I had come from another world more than twenty-six million miles from his familiar Amtor, which is the name by which the Venusans know their world, he shook his head skeptically.

"There is no life beyond Amtor," he said. "How can there be life where all is fire?"

"What is your theory of the—" I started, but had to stop. There is no Amtorian word for universe, neither is there any for sun, moon, star, or planet. The gorgeous heavens that we see are never seen by the inhabitants of Venus, obscured as they perpetually are by the two great cloud envelopes that surround the planet." I started over again. "What do you believe surrounds Amtor?" I asked.

He stepped to a shelf and returned with a large volume, which he opened at a beautifully executed map of Amtor. It showed three concentric circles. Between the two inner circles lay a circular belt designated as Trabol, which means warm country. Here the boundaries of seas, continents, and islands were traced to the edges of the two circles that bounded it, in some places crossing these boundaries as though marking the spots at which venturesome explorers had dared the perils of an unknown and inhospitable land.

"This is Trabol," explained Danus, placing a finger upon that portion of the map I have briefly described. "It entirely surrounds Strabol, which lies in the center of Amtor. Strabol is extremely hot, its land is covered with enormous forests and dense undergrowth, and is peopled by huge land animals, reptiles, and birds, its warm seas swarm with monsters of the deep. No man has ventured far into Strabol and lived to return.

"Beyond Trabol," he continued, placing his finger on the outer band designated as Karbol (Cold Country), "lies Karbol. Here it is as cold as Strabol is hot. There are strange animals there too, and adventurers have returned with tales of fierce human beings clothed in fur. But it is an inhospitable land into which there is no occasion to venture and which few dare penetrate far for fear of being precipitated over the rim into the molten sea."

"Over what rim?" I asked.

He looked at me in astonishment. "I can well believe that you come from another world when you ask me such questions as you do," he remarked. "Do you mean to tell me that you know nothing of the physical structure of Amtor?"

"I know nothing of your theory concerning it," I replied.

"It is not a theory; it is a fact," he corrected me gently. "In no other way may the various phenomena of nature be explained. Amtor is a huge disc with an upturned rim, like a great saucer; it floats upon a sea of molten metal and rock, a fact that is incontrovertably proved by the gushing forth of this liquid mass occasionally from the summits of mountains, when a hole has been burned in the bottom of Amtor. Karbol, the cold country, is a wise provision of nature that tempers the terrific heat that must constantly surge about the outer rim of Amtor.

"Above Amtor, and entirely surrounding her above the molten sea, is a chaos of fire and flame. From this our clouds protect us. Occasionally there have occurred rifts in the clouds, and at such times the heat from the fires above, when the rifts occurred in the daytime, has been so intense as to wither vegetation and destroy life, while the light that shone through was of blinding intensity. When these rifts occurred at night there was no heat, but we saw the sparks from the fire shining above us."

I tried to explain the spherical shape of the planets and that Karbol was only the colder country surrounding one of Amtor's poles, while Strabol, the hot country, lay in the equatorial region; that Trabol was merely one of two temperate zones, the other one being beyond the equatorial region, which was a band around the middle of a globe and not, as he supposed, a circular area in the center of a disc. He listened to me politely, but only smiled and shook his head when I had finished.

At first I could not comprehend that a man of such evident intelligence, education, and culture should cling to such a belief as his, but when I stopped to consider the fact that neither he nor any of his progenitors had ever seen the heavens, I began to realize that there could not be much foundation for any other theory, and even theories must have foundations. I also realized, even more than I had before, something of what astronomy has meant to the human race of earth in the advancement of science and civilization. Could there have been such advancement had the heavens been perpetually hidden from our view? I wonder.

But I did not give up. I drew his attention to the fact that if his theory were correct, the boundary between Trabol and Strabol (the temperate and the equatorial zones) should be much shorter than that separating Trabol from Karbol, the polar region, as was shown on the map, but could not have been proved by actual survey; while my theory would require that the exact opposite be true, which was easily demonstrable and must have been demonstrated if surveys had ever been made, which I judged from the markings on the map to be the case.

He admitted that surveys had been made and that they had shown the apparent discrepancy that I had pointed out, but he explained this ingeniously by a purely Amtorian theory of the relativity of distance, which he proceeded to elucidate.

"A degree is one thousandth part of the circumference of a circle," he commenced. (This is the Amtorian degree, her savants not having had the advantage of a visible sun to suggest another division of the circumference of a circle as did the Babylonians, who hit upon three hundred sixty as being close enough.) "And no matter what the length of the circumference, it measures just one thousand degrees. The circle which separates Strabol from Trabol is necessarily one thousand degrees in length. You will admit that?"

"Certainly," I replied.

"Very good! Then, will you admit that the circle which separates Trabol from Karbol measures exactly one thousand degrees?"

I nodded my assent.

"Things which equal the same thing equal each other, do they not? Therefore, the inner and outer boundaries of Trabol are of equal length, and this is true because of the truth of the theory of relativity of distance. The degree is our unit of linear measure. It would be ridiculous to say that the farther one was removed from the center of Amtor the longer the unit of distance became; it only appears to become longer; in relation to the circumference of the circle and in relation to the distance from the center of Amtor it is precisely the same.

"I know," he admitted, "that on the map it does not appear to be the same, nor do actual surveys indicate that it is the same; but it must be the same, for if it were not, it is obvious that Amtor would be larger around the closer one approached the center and smallest of all at the perimeter, which is so obviously ridiculous as to require no refutation.

"This seeming discrepancy caused the ancients considerable perturbation until about three thousand years ago, when Klufar, the great scientist, expounded the theory of relativity of distance and demonstrated that the real and apparent measurements of distance could be reconciled by multiplying each by the square root of minus one."

I saw that argument was useless and said no more; there is no use arguing with a man who can multiply anything by the square root of minus one.

CHAPTER FIVE

The Girl in the Garden

For some time I had been aware that I was in the house of Mintep, the king, and that the country was called Vepaja. Jong, which I had originally thought to be his name, was his title; it is Amtorian for king. I learned that Duran was of the house of Zar and that Olthar and Kamlot were his sons; Zuro, one of the women I had met there, was attached to Duran; the other, Alzo, was attached to Olthar; Kamlot had no woman. I use the word attached partially because it is a reasonably close translation of the Amtorian word for the connection and partially because no other word seems exactly to explain the relationship between these men and women.

They were not married, because the institution of marriage is unknown here. One could not say that they belonged to the men, because they were in no sense slaves or servants, nor had they been acquired by purchase or feat of arms. They had come willingly, following a courtship, and they were free to depart whenever they chose, just as the men were free to depart and seek other connections; but, as I was to learn later, these connections are seldom broken, while infidelity is as rare here as it is prevalent on earth.

Each day I took exercise on the broad veranda that encircled the tree at the level upon which my apartment was located; at least, I assumed that it encircled the tree, but I did not know, as that portion assigned to me was but a hundred feet long, a fifteenth part of the circumference of the great tree. At each end of my little segment was a fence. The section adjoining mine on the right appeared to be a garden, as it was a mass of flowers and shrubbery growing in soil that must have been brought up from that distant surface of the planet that I had as yet neither set foot upon nor seen. The section on my left extended in front of the quarters of several young officers attached to the household of the king. I call them young because Danus told me they were young, but they appear to be about the same age as all the other Amtorians I have seen. They were pleasant fellows, and after I learned to speak their language we occasionally had friendly chats together.

But in the section at my right I had never seen a human being; and then one day, when Danus was absent and I was walking alone, I saw a girl among the flowers there. She did not see me; and I only caught the briefest glimpse of her, but there was something about her that made me want to see her again, and thereafter I rather neglected the young officers on my left.

Though I haunted the end of my veranda next the garden for several days, I did not again see the girl during all that time. The place seemed utterly deserted until one day I saw the figure of a man among the shrubbery. He was moving with great caution, creeping stealthily; and presently, behind him, I saw another and another, until I had counted five of them all together.

They were similar to the Vepajans, yet there was a difference. They appeared coarser, more brutal, than any of the men I had as yet seen; and in other ways they were dissimilar to Danus, Duran, Kamlot, and my other Venusan acquaintances. There was something menacing and sinister, too, in their silent, stealthy movements.

I wondered what they were doing there; and then I thought of the girl, and for some reason the conclusion was forced upon me that the presence of these men here had something to do with her, and that it boded her harm. Just in what way I could not even surmise, knowing so little of the people among whom fate had thrown me; but the impression was quite definite, and it excited me. Perhaps it rather overcame my better judgment, too, if my next act is any index to the matter.

Without thought of the consequences and in total ignorance of the identity of the men or the purpose for which they were in the garden, I vaulted the low fence and followed them. I made no noise. They had not seen me originally because I had been hidden from their view by a larger shrub that grew close to the fence that separated the garden from my veranda. It was through the foliage of this shrub that I had observed them, myself unobserved.

Moving cautiously but swiftly, I soon overtook the hindmost man and saw that the five were moving toward an open doorway beyond which, in a richly furnished apartment, I saw the girl who had aroused my curiosity and whose beautiful face had led me into this mad adventure. Almost simultaneously, the girl glanced up and saw the leading man at the doorway. She screamed, and then I knew that I had not come in vain.

Instantly I leaped upon the man in front of me, and as I did so I gave a great shout, hoping by that means to distract the attention of the other four from the girl to me, and in that I was wholly successful. The other four turned instantly. I had taken my man so completely by surprise that I was able to snatch his sword from its scabbard before he could recover his wits; and as he drew his dagger and struck at me, I ran his own blade through his heart; then the others were upon me.

Their faces were contorted by rage, and I could see that they would give me no quarter.

The narrow spaces between the shrubbery reduced the advantage which four men would ordinarily have had over a single antagonist, for they could attack me only singly; but I knew what the outcome must eventually be if help did not reach me, and as my only goal was to keep the men from the girl, I backed slowly toward the fence and my own veranda as I saw that all four of the men were following me.

My shout and the girl's scream had attracted attention; and presently I heard men running in the apartment in which I had seen the girl, and her voice directing them toward the garden. I hoped they would come before the fellows had backed me against the wall, where I was confident that I must go down in defeat beneath four swords wielded by men more accustomed to them than I. I thanked the good fortune, however, that had led me to take up fencing seriously in Germany, for it was helping me now, though I could not long hold out against these men with the Venusan sword which was a new weapon to me.

I had reached the fence at last and was fighting with my back toward it. The fellow facing me was cutting viciously at me. I could hear the men coming from the apartment. Could I hold out? Then my opponent swung a terrific cut at my head, and, instead of parrying it, I leaped to one side and simultaneously stepped in and cut at him. His own swing had carried him off balance, and, of course, his guard was down. My blade cut deep into his neck, severing his jugular. From behind him another man was rushing upon me.

Relief was coming. The girl was safe. I could accomplish no more by remaining there and being cut to pieces, a fate I had only narrowly averted in the past few seconds. I hurled my sword, point first, at the oncoming Venusan; and as it tore into his breast I turned and vaulted the fence into my own veranda.

Then, as I looked back, I saw a dozen Vepajan warriors overwhelm the two remaining intruders, butchering them like cattle. There was no shouting and no sound other than the brief clash of swords as the two sought desperately but futilely to defend themselves. The Vepajans spoke no word. They seemed shocked and terrified, though their terror had most certainly not been the result of any fear of their late antagonists. There was something else which I did not understand, something mysterious in their manner, their silence, and their actions immediately following the encounter.

Quickly they seized the bodies of the five strange warriors that had been killed and, carrying them to the outer garden wall, hurled them over into that bottomless abyss of the forest the terrific depths of which my eyes had never been able to plumb. Then, in equal silence, they departed from the garden by the same path by which they had entered it.

I realized that they had not seen me, and I knew that the girl had not. I wondered a little how they accounted for the deaths of the three men I had disposed of, but I never learned. The whole affair was a mystery to me and was only explained long after in the light of ensuing events.

I thought that Danus might mention it and thus give me an opportunity to question him; but he never did, and something kept me from broaching the subject to him, modesty perhaps. In other respects, however, my curiosity concerning these people was insatiable; and I fear that I bored Danus to the verge of distraction with my incessant questioning, but I excused myself on the plea that I could only learn the language by speaking it and hearing it spoken; and Danus, that most delightful of men, insisted that it was not only a pleasure to inform me but his duty as well, the jong having requested him to inform me fully concerning the life, customs, and history of the Vepajans.

One of the many things that puzzled me was why such an intelligent and cultured people should be living in trees, apparently without servants or slaves and with no intercourse, as far as I had been able to discover, with other peoples; so one evening I asked him.

"It is a long story," replied Danus; "much of it you will find in the histories here upon my shelves, but I can give you a brief outline that will at least answer your question.

"Hundreds of years ago the kings of Vepaja ruled a great country. It was not this forest island where you now find us, but a broad empire that embraced a thousand islands and extended from Strabol to Karbol; it included broad land masses and great oceans; it was graced by mighty cities and boasted a wealth and commerce unsurpassed through all the centuries before or since.

"The people of Vepaja in those days were numbered in the millions; there were millions of merchants and millions of wage earners and millions of slaves, and there was a smaller class of brain workers. This class included the learned professions of science, medicine, and law, of letters and the creative arts. The military leaders were selected from all classes. Over all was the hereditary jong.

"The lines between the classes were neither definitely nor strictly drawn; a slave might become a free man, a free man might become anything he chose within the limits of his ability, short of jong. In social intercourse the four principal classes did not intermingle with each other, due to the fact that members of one class had little in common with members of the other classes and not through any feeling of superiority or inferiority. When a member of a lower class had won by virtue of culture, learning, or genius to a position in a higher class, he was received upon an equal footing, and no thought was given to his antecedents.

"Vepaja was prosperous and happy, yet there were malcontents. These were the lazy and incompetent. Many of them were of the criminal class. They were envious of those who had won to positions which they were not mentally equipped to attain. Over a long period of time they were responsible for minor discord and dissension, but the people either paid no attention to them or laughed them down. Then they found a leader. He was a laborer named Thor, a man with a criminal record.

"This man founded a secret order known as Thorists and preached a gospel of class hatred called Thorism. By means of lying propaganda he gained a large following, and as all his energies were directed against a single class, he had all the vast millions of the other three classes to draw from, though naturally he found few converts among the merchants and employers which also included the agrarian class.

"The sole end of the Thorist leaders was personal power and aggrandizement; their aims were wholly selfish, yet, because they worked solely among the ignorant masses, they had little difficulty in deceiving their dupes, who finally rose under their false leaders in a bloody revolution that sounded the doom of the civilization and advancement of a world.

"Their purpose was the absolute destruction of the cultured class. Those of the other classes who opposed them were to be subjugated or destroyed; the jong and his family were to be killed. These things accomplished, the people would enjoy absolute freedom; there would be no masters, no taxes, no laws.

"They succeeded in killing most of us and a large proportion of the merchant class; then the people discovered what the agitators already knew, that someone must rule, and the leaders of Thorism were ready to take over the reins of government. The people had exchanged the beneficent rule of an experienced and cultured class for that of greedy incompetents and theorists.

"Now they are all reduced to virtual slavery. An army of spies watches over them, and an army of warriors keeps them from turning against their masters; they are miserable, helpless, and hopeless.

"Those of us who escaped with our jong sought out this distant, uninhabited island. Here we constructed tree cities, such as this, far above the ground, from which they cannot be seen. We brought our culture with us and little else; but our wants are few, and we are happy. We would not return to the old system if we might. We have learned our lesson, that a people divided amongst themselves cannot be happy. Where there are even slight class distinctions there are envy and jealousy. Here there are none; we are all of the same class. We have no servants; whatever there is to do we do better than servants ever did it. Even those who serve the jong are not servants in the sense that they are menials, for their positions are considered posts of honor, and the greatest among us take turns in filling them."

"But I still do not understand why you choose to live in trees, far above the ground," I said.

"For years the Thorists hunted us down to kill us," he explained, "and we were forced to live in hidden, inaccessible places; this type of city was the solution of our problem. The Thorists still hunt us; and there are still occasional raids, but now they are for a very different purpose. Instead of wishing to kill us, they now wish to capture as many of us as they can.

"Having killed or driven away the brains of the nation, their civilization has deteriorated, disease is making frightful inroads upon them which they are unable to check, old age has reappeared and is taking its toll; so they seek to capture the brains and the skill and the knowledge which they have been unable to produce and which we alone possess."

"Old age is reappearing! What do you mean?" I asked.

"Have you not noticed that there are no signs of old age among us?" he inquired.

"Yes, of course," I replied, "nor any children. I have often meant to ask you for an explanation."

"These are not natural phenomena," he assured me; "they are the crowning achievements of medical science. A thousand years ago the serum of longevity was perfected. It is injected every two years and not only provides immunity from all diseases but insures the complete restoration of all wasted tissue.

"But even in good there is evil. As none grew old and none died, except those who met with violent deaths, we were faced with the grave dangers of overpopulation. To combat this, birth control became obligatory. Children are permitted now only in sufficient numbers to replace actual losses in population. If a member of a house is killed, a woman of that house is permitted to bear a child, if she can; but after generations of childlessness there is a constantly decreasing number of women who are capable of bearing children. This situation we have met by anticipating it.

"Statistics compiled over a period of a thousand years indicate the average death rate expectancy per thousand people; they have also demonstrated that only fifty per cent of our women are capable of bearing children; therefore, fifty per cent of the required children are permitted yearly to those who wish them, in the order in which their applications are filed."

"I have not seen a child since I arrived in Amtor," I told him.

"There are children here," he replied, "but, of course, not many."

"And no old people," I mused. "Could you administer that serum to me, Danus?"

He smiled. "With Mintep's permission, which I imagine will not be difficult to obtain. Come," he added, "I'll take some blood tests now to determine the type and attenuation of serum best adapted to your requirements." He motioned me into his laboratory.

When he had completed the tests, which he accomplished with ease and rapidity, he was shocked by the variety and nature of malignant bacteria they revealed.

"You are a menace to the continued existence of human life on Amtor," he exclaimed with a laugh.

"I am considered a very healthy man in my own world," I assured him.

"How old are you?" he asked.

"Twenty-seven."

"You would not be so healthy two hundred years from now if all those bacteria were permitted to have their way with you."

"How old might I live to be if they were eradicated?" I asked.

He shrugged. "We do not know. The serum was perfected a thousand years ago. There are people among us today who were of the first to receive injections. I am over five hundred years old; Mintep is seven hundred. We believe that, barring accidents, we shall live forever; but, of course, we do not know. Theoretically, we should."

He was called away at this juncture; and I went out on the veranda to take my exercise, of which I have found that I require a great deal, having always been athletically inclined. Swimming, boxing, and wrestling had strengthened and developed my muscles since I had returned to America with my mother when I was eleven, and I became interested in fencing while I was travelling in Europe after she died. During my college days I was amateur middleweight boxer of California, and I captured several medals for distance swimming; so the inforced inactivity of the past two months had galled me considerably. Toward the end of my college days I had grown into the heavyweight class, but that had been due to an increase of healthy bone and sinew; now I was at least twenty pounds heavier and that twenty pounds was all fat.

On my one hundred feet of veranda I did the best I could to reduce. I ran miles, I shadow boxed, I skipped rope, and I spent hours with the old seventeen setting-up exercises of drill regulations. Today I was shadow boxing near the right end of my veranda when I suddenly discovered the girl in the garden observing me. As our eyes met I halted in my tracks and smiled at her. A frightened look came into her eyes, and she turned and fled. I wondered why.

Puzzled, I walked slowly back toward my apartment, my exercises forgotten. This time I had seen the girl's full face, looked her squarely in the eyes, and I had been absolutely dumfounded by her beauty. Every man and woman I had seen since I had come to Venus had been beautiful; I had come to expect that. But I had not expected to see in this or any other world such indescribable perfection of coloring and features, combined with character and intelligence, as that which I had just seen in the garden beyond my little fence. But why had she run away when I smiled?

Possibly she had run away merely because she had been discovered watching me for, after all, human nature is about the same everywhere. Even twenty-six million miles from earth there are human beings like ourselves and a girl, with quite human curiosity, who runs away when she is discovered. I wondered if she resembled earthly girls in other respects, but she seemed too beautiful to be just like anything on earth or in heaven. Was she young or old? Suppose she were seven hundred years old!

I went to my apartment and prepared to bathe and change my loincloth; I had long since adopted the apparel of Amtor. As I glanced in a mirror that hangs in my bathroom I suddenly understood why the girl may have looked frightened and run away—my beard! It was nearly a month old now and might easily have frightened anyone who had never before seen a beard.

When Danus returned I asked him what I could do about it. He stepped into another room and returned with a bottle of salve.

"Rub this into the roots of the hair on your face," he directed, "but be careful not to get it on your eyebrows, lashes, or the hair on your head. Leave it there a minute and then wash your face."

I stepped into my bathroom and opened the jar; its contents looked like vaseline and smelled like the devil, but I rubbed it into the roots of my beard as Danus had directed. When I washed my face a moment later my beard came off, leaving my face smooth and hairless. I hurried back to the room where I had left Danus.

"You are quite handsome after all," he remarked. "Do all the people of this fabulous world of which you have told me have hair growing on their faces?"

"Nearly all," I replied, "but in my country the majority of men keep it shaved off."

"I should think the women would be the ones to shave," he commented. "A woman with hair on her face would be quite repulsive to an Amtorian."

"But our women do not have hair on their faces," I assured him.

"And the men do! A fabulous world indeed."

"But if Amtorians do not grow beards, what was the need of this salve that you gave me?" I asked.

"It was perfected as an aid to surgery," he explained. "In treating scalp wounds and in craniectomies it is necessary to remove the hair from about the wound. This unguent serves the purpose better than shaving and also retards the growth of new hair for a longer time."

"But the hair will grow out again?" I asked.

"Yes, if you do not apply the unguent too frequently," he replied.

"How frequently?" I demanded.

"Use it every day for six days and the hair will never again grow on your face. We used to use it on the heads of confirmed criminals. Whenever one saw a bald-headed man or a man wearing a wig he watched his valuables."

"In my country when one sees a bald-headed man," I said, "he watches his girls. And that reminds me; I have seen a beautiful girl in a garden just to the right of us here. Who is she?"

"She is one whom you are not supposed to see, he replied. "Were I you, I should not again mention the fact that you have seen her. Did she see you?"

"She saw me," I replied.

"What did she do?" His tone was serious.

"She appeared frightened and ran."

"Perhaps you had best keep away from that end of the veranda," he suggested.

There was that in his manner which precluded questions, and I did not pursue the subject further. Here was a mystery, the first suggestion of mystery that I had encountered in the life of Vepaja, and naturally it piqued my curiosity. Why should I not look at the girl? I had looked at other women without incurring displeasure. Was it only this particular girl upon whom I must not look, or were there other girls equally sacrosanct? It occurred to me that she might be a priestess of some holy order, but I was forced to discard that theory because of my belief that these people had no religion, at least none that I could discover in my talks with Danus. I had attempted to describe some of our earthly religious beliefs to him, but he simply could not perceive either their purpose or meaning any more than he could visualize the solar system of the universe.

Having once seen the girl, I was anxious to see her again; and now that the thing was proscribed, I was infinitely more desirous than ever to look upon her divine loveliness and to speak with her. I had not promised Danus that I would heed his suggestions, for I was determined to ignore them should the opportunity arise.

I was commencing to tire of the virtual imprisonment that had been my lot ever since my advent upon Amtor, for even a kindly jailer and a benign prison régime are not satisfactory substitutes for freedom. I had asked Danus what my status was and what they planned for me in the future, but he had evaded a more direct answer by saying that I was the guest of Mintep, the jong, and that my future would be a matter of discussion when Mintep granted me an audience.

Suddenly now I felt more than before the restrictions of my situation, and they galled me. I had committed no crime. I was a peaceful visitor to Vepaja. I had neither the desire nor the power to harm anyone. These considerations decided me. I determined to force the issue.

A few minutes ago I had been contented with my lot, willing to wait the pleasure of my hosts; now I was discontented. What had induced this sudden change? Could it be the mysterious alchemy of personality that had transmuted the lead of lethargy to the gold of ambitious desire? Had the aura of a vision of feminine loveliness thus instantly reversed my outlook upon life?

I turned toward Danus. "You have been very kind to me," I said, "and my days here have been happy, but I am of a race of people who desire freedom above all things. As I have explained to you, I am here through no intentional fault of my own; but I am here, and being here I expect the same treatment that would be accorded you were you to visit my country under similar circumstances."

"And what treatment would that be?" he asked.

"The right to life, liberty, and the pursuit of happiness—freedom," I explained. I did not think it necessary to mention chambers of commerce dinners, Rotary and Kiwanis luncheons, triumphal parades and ticker tape, keys to cities, press representatives and photographers, nor news reel cameramen, the price that he would undoubtedly have had to pay for life, liberty, and the pursuit of happiness.

"But, my dear friend, one would think from your words that you are a prisoner here!" he exclaimed.

"I am, Danus," I replied, "and none knows it better than you."

He shrugged. "I am sorry that you feel that way about it, Carson."

"How much longer is it going to last?" I demanded.

"The jong is the jong," he replied. "He will send for you in his own time; until then, let us continue the friendly relations that have marked our association up to now."

"I hope they will never be changed, Danus," I told him, "but you may tell Mintep, if you will, that I cannot accept his hospitality much longer; if he does not send for me soon, I shall leave on my own accord."

"Do not attempt that, my friend," he warned me.

"And why not?"

"You would not live to take a dozen steps from the apartments that have been assigned you," he assured me seriously.

"Who would stop me?"

"There are warriors posted in the corridors," he explained; "they have their orders from the jong."

"And yet I am not a prisoner!" I exclaimed with a bitter laugh.

"I am sorry that you raised the question," he said, "as otherwise you might never have known."

Here indeed was the iron hand in the velvet glove. I hoped it was not wielded by a wolf in sheep's clothing. My position was not an enviable one. Even had I the means to escape, there was no place that I could go. But I did not want to leave Vepaja—I had seen the girl in the garden.

CHAPTER SIX

Gathering Tarel

A week passed, a week during which I permanently discarded my reddish whiskers and received an injection of the longevity serum. The latter event suggested that possibly Mintep would eventually liberate me, for why bestow immortality upon a potential enemy who is one's prisoner; but then I knew that the serum did not confer absolute immortality—Mintep could have me destroyed if he wished, by which thought was suggested the possibility that the serum had been administered for the purpose of lulling me into a sense of security which I did not, in reality, enjoy. I was becoming suspicious.

While Danus was injecting the serum, I asked him if there were many doctors in Vepaja. "Not so many in proportion to the population as there were a thousand years ago," he replied. "All the people are now trained in the care of their bodies and taught the essentials of health and longevity. Even without the serums we use to maintain resistance to disease constantly in the human body, our people would live to great ages. Sanitation, diet, and exercise can accomplish wonders by themselves.

"But we must have some doctors. Their numbers are limited now to about one to each five thousand citizens, and in addition to administering the serum, the doctors attend those who are injured by the accidents of daily life, in the hunt, and in duels and war.

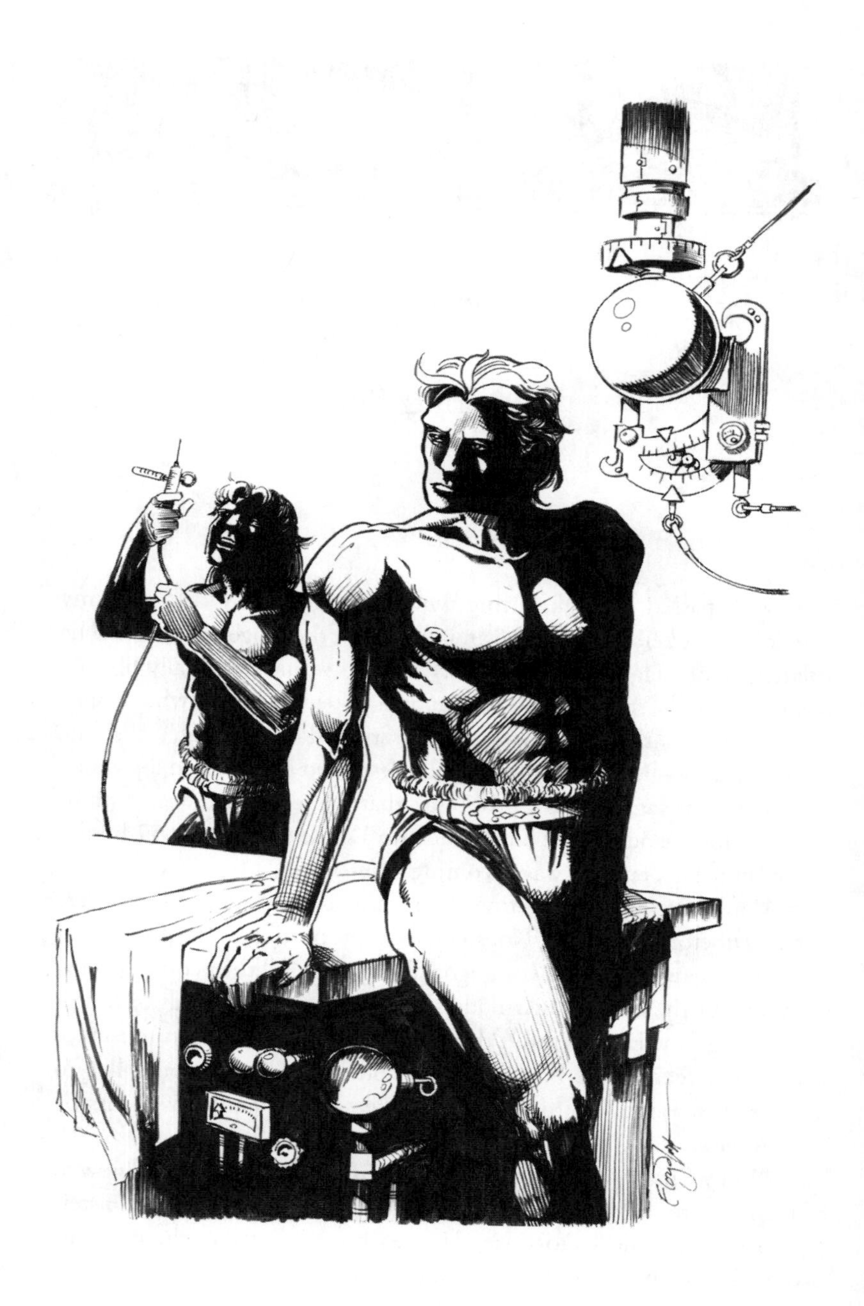

"Formerly there were many more doctors than could eke out an honest living, but now there are various agencies that restrict their numbers. Not only is there a law restricting these, but the ten years of study required, the long apprenticeship thereafter, and the difficult examinations that must be passed have all tended to reduce the numbers who seek to follow this profession; but another factor probably achieved more than all else to rapidly reduce the great number of doctors that threatened the continuance of human life on Amtor in the past.

"This was a regulation that compelled every physician and surgeon to file a complete history of each of his cases with the chief medical officer of his district. From diagnosis to complete recovery or death, each detail of the handling of each case had to be recorded and placed on record for the public to consult. When a citizen requires the services of a physician or surgeon now, he may easily determine those who have been successful and those who have not. Fortunately, today there are few of the latter. The law has proved a good one."

This was interesting, for I had had experience with physicians and surgeons on earth. "How many doctors survived the operation of this new law?" I asked.

"About two per cent," he replied.

"There must have been a larger proportion of good doctors on Amtor than on earth," I commented.

Time hung heavily upon my hands. I read a great deal, but an active young man cannot satisfy all his varied life interests with books alone. And then there was the garden at my right. I had been advised to avoid that end of my veranda, but I did not, at least not when Danus was absent. When he was away I haunted that end of the veranda, but it seemed deserted. And then one day I caught a glimpse of her; she was watching me from behind a flowering shrub.

I was close to the fence that separated my runway from her garden; it was not a high fence, perhaps slightly under five feet. She did not run this time, but stood looking straight at me, possibly thinking that I could not see her because of the intervening foliage. I could not see her plainly enough, that is true; and, God, how I wanted to see her!

What is that inexplicable, subtle attraction that some woman holds for every man? For some men there is only one woman in the world who exercises this influence upon him, or perhaps if there are more, the others do not cross his path; for other men there are several; for some none. For me there was this girl of an alien race, upon an alien planet. Perhaps there were others, but if there were, I had never met them. In all my life before I had never been moved by such an irresistible urge. What I did, I did upon the strength of an impulse as uncontrollable as a law of nature; perhaps it was a law of nature that motivated me. I vaulted the fence.

Before the girl could escape me, I stood before her. There were consternation and horror in her eyes. I thought that she was afraid of me.

"Do not be afraid," I said; "I have not come to harm you, only to speak to you."

She drew herself up proudly. "I am not afraid of you," she said; "I—," she hesitated and then started over. "If you are seen here you will be destroyed. Go back to your quarters at once and never dare such a rash act again."

I thrilled to the thought that the fear that I had seen so clearly reflected in her eyes was for my safety. "How may I see you?" I asked.

"You may never see me," she replied.

"But I have seen you, and I intend seeing you again. I am going to see a lot of you, or die in the attempt."

"Either you do not know what you are doing or you are mad," she said and turned her back on me as she started to walk away.

I seized her arm. "Wait," I begged.

She wheeled on me like a tigress and slapped my face, and then she whipped the dagger from the scabbard at her girdle. "How dared you," she cried, "lay a hand upon me! I should kill you."

"Why don't you?" I asked.

"I loathe you," she said, and it sounded as though she meant it.

"I love you," I replied, and I knew that I spoke the truth.

At that declaration her eyes did indeed reflect horror. She wheeled then so quickly that I could not stop her and was gone. I stood for a moment, debating whether I should follow her or not, and then a modicum of reason intervened to save me from such an assininity. An instant later I had vaulted the fence again. I did not know whether anyone had seen me or not, and I did not care.

When Danus returned a short time later, he told me that Mintep had sent him for me. I wondered if the summons was in any way related to my adventure in the garden at the right, but I did not inquire. If it were, I should know in due time. The attitude of Danus was unchanged, but that no longer reassured me. I was beginning to suspect that the Amtorians were masters of dissimulation.

Two young officers from the quarters adjoining mine accompanied us to the chamber where the jong was to question me. Whether or not they were acting as an escort to prevent my escape I could not tell. They chatted pleasantly with me during the short walk along the corridor and up the staircase to the level above; but then the guards usually chat pleasantly with the condemned man, if he feels like chatting. They accompanied me into the room where the jong sat. This time he was not alone; there were a number of men gathered about him, and among these I recognized Duran, Olthar, and Kamlot. For some reason the assemblage reminded me of a grand jury, and I could not help but wonder if they were going to return a true bill.

I bowed to the jong, who greeted me quite pleasantly enough, and smiled and nodded to the three men in whose home I had spent my first night on Venus. Mintep looked me over in silence for a moment or two; when he had seen me before I had been dressed in my earthly clothes, now I was garbed (or ungarbed) like a Vepajan.

"Your skin is not as light in color as I thought it," he commented.

"Exposure to light on the veranda has darkened it," I replied. I could not say sunlight, because they have no word for sun, of the existence of which they do not dream. However, such was the case, the ultra violet rays of sunlight having penetrated the cloud envelopes surrounding the planet and tanned my body quite as effectively as would exposure to the direct rays of the sun have done.

"You have been quite happy here, I trust," he said.

"I have been treated with kindness and consideration," I replied, "and have been quite as happy as any prisoner could reasonably be expected to be."

The shadow of a smile touched his lips. "You are candid," he commented.

"Candor is a characteristic of the country from which I come," I replied.

"However, I do not like the word prisoner," he said.

"Neither do I, jong, but I like the truth. I have been a prisoner, and I have been awaiting this opportunity to ask you why I am a prisoner and to demand my freedom."

He raised his eyebrows; then he smiled quite openly. "I think that I am going to like you," he said; "you are honest and you are courageous, or I am no judge of men."

I inclined my head in acknowledgment of the compliment. I had not expected that he would receive my blunt demand in a spirit of such generous understanding; but I was not entirely relieved, for experience had taught me that these people could be very suave while being most uncompromising.

"There are some things that I wish to tell you and some questions that I wish to ask you," he continued. "We are still beset by our enemies, who yet send occasional raiding parties against us, who upon numerous occasions have sought to introduce their spies among us. We have three things that they require if they are not to suffer extinction: scientific knowledge, and the brains and experience to apply it. Therefore they go to any lengths to abduct our men, whom they purpose holding in slavery and forcing to apply the knowledge that they themselves do not have. They also abduct our women in the hope of breeding children of greater mentality than those which are now born to them.

"The story that you told of crossing millions of miles of space from another world is, of course, preposterous and naturally aroused our suspicions. We saw in you another Thorist spy, cleverly disguised. For this reason you have been under the careful and intelligent observation of Danus for many days. He reports that there is no doubt but that you were totally ignorant of the Amtorian language when you came among us, and as this is the only language spoken by any of the known races of the world, we have come to the conclusion that your story may be, in part, true. The fact that your skin, hair, and eyes differ in color from those of any known race is further substantiation of this conclusion.

Therefore, we are willing to admit that you are not a Thorist, but the questions remain: who are you, and from whence came you?"

"I have told only the truth," I replied; "I have nothing to add other than to suggest that you carefully consider the fact that the cloud masses surrounding Amtor completely obscure your view and therefore your knowledge of what lies beyond."

He shook his head. "Let us not discuss it; it is useless to attempt to overthrow the accumulated scientific research and knowledge of thousands of years. We are willing to accept you as of another race, perhaps, as was suggested by the clothing you wore upon your arrival, from cold and dreary Karbol. You are free to come and go as you please. If you remain, you must abide by the laws and customs of Vepaja, and you must become self-supporting. What can you do?"

"I doubt that I can compete with Vepajans at their own trades or professions," I admitted, "but I can learn something if I am given time."

"Perhaps we can find someone who will undertake your training," said the jong, "and in the meantime you may remain in my house, assisting Danus."

"We will take him into our house and train him," spoke up Duran, "if he cares to help us collect tarel and hunt."

Tarel is the strong, silky fiber from which their cloth and cordage are made. I imagined that collecting it would be tame and monotonous work, but the idea of hunting appealed to me. In no event, however, could I ignore Duran's well-meant invitation, as I did not wish to offend him, and, furthermore, anything would be acceptable that would provide the means whereby I might become self-supporting. I therefore accepted his offer, and, the audience being concluded, I bid good-bye to Danus, who invited me to visit him often, and withdrew with Duran, Olthar, and Kamlot.

As no mention had been made of the subject, I concluded that no one had witnessed my encounter with the girl in the garden, who was still uppermost in my thoughts and the principal cause of my regret that I was to leave the house of the jong.

Once more I was established in the house of Duran, but this time in a larger and more comfortable room. Kamlot took charge of me. He was the younger of the brothers, a quiet, reserved man with the muscular development of a trained athlete. After he had shown me my room, he took me to another apartment, a miniature armory, in which were many spears, swords, daggers, bows, shields, and almost countless arrows. Before a window was a long bench with racks in which were tools of various descriptions; above the bench were shelves upon which were stacked the raw materials for the manufacture of bows, arrows, and spear shafts. Near the bench were a forge and anvil, and there were sheets and rods and ingots of metal stored near by.

"Have you ever used a sword?" he asked as he selected one for me.

"Yes, but for exercise only," I replied; "in my country we have perfected weapons that render a sword useless in combat."

He asked me about these weapons and was much interested in my description of earthly firearms. "We have a similar weapon on Amtor, he said. "We of Vepaja do not possess them, because the sole supply of the material with which they are charged lies in the heart of the Thorist country. When the weapons are made they are charged with an element that emits a ray of extremely short wave length that is destructive of animal tissue, but the element only emits these rays when exposed to the radiation of another rare element. There are several metals that are impervious to these rays. Those shields that you see hanging on the walls, the ones that are metal covered, are ample protection from them. A small shutter of similar metal is used in the weapon to separate the two elements; when this shutter is raised and one element is exposed to the emanations of the other, the destructive R-ray is released and passes along the bore of the weapon toward the target at which the latter has been aimed.

"My people invented and perfected this weapon," he added ruefully, "and now it has been turned against us; but we get along very well with what we have, as long as we remain in our trees.

"In addition to a sword and dagger, you will need a bow, arrows, and a spear," and as he enumerated them he selected the various articles for me, the last of which was really a short, heavy javelin. A swivelled ring was attached to the end of the shaft of this weapon, and attached to the ring was a long, slender cord with a hand loop at its extremity. This cord, which was no heavier than ordinary wrapping twine, Kamlot coiled in a peculiar way and tucked into a small opening in the side of the shaft.

"What is the purpose of that cord?" I asked, examining the weapon.

"We hunt high in the trees," he replied, "and if it were not for the cord we should lose many spears."

"But that cord is not heavy enough for that, is it?" I asked.

"It is of tarel," he replied, "and could support the weight of ten men. You will learn much of the properties and value of tarel before you have been with us long. Tomorrow we shall go out together and gather some. It has been rather scarce of late."

At the evening meal that day I met Zuro and Alzo again, and they were most gracious to me. In the evening they all joined in teaching me the favorite Vepajan game, tork, which is played with pieces that are much like those used in mah jong and bears a startling resemblance to poker.

I slept well that night in my new quarters and when daylight broke I arose, for Kamlot had warned me that we should start early upon our expedition. I cannot say that I looked forward with any considerable degree of enthusiasm to spending the day gathering tarel. The climate of Vepaja is warm and sultry, and I pictured the adventure as being about as monotonous and disagreeable as picking cotton in Imperial Valley.

After a light breakfast, which I helped Kamlot prepare, he told me to get my weapons. "You should always wear your sword and dagger," he added.

"Even in the house?" I asked.

"Always, wherever you are," he replied. "It is not only a custom, but it is the law. We never know when we may be called upon to defend ourselves, our houses, or our jong."

"Those are all that I need bring, I suppose," I remarked as I was leaving the room.

"Bring your spear, of course; we are going to gather tarel," he replied.

Why I should need a spear to gather tarel I could not imagine; but I brought all the weapons that he had mentioned, and when I returned he handed me a bag with a strap that went around my neck to support it at my back.

"Is this for the tarel?" I asked.

He replied that it was.

"You do not expect to gather much," I remarked.

"We may not get any," he replied. "If we get a bagful between us we may do some tall boasting when we return."

I said no more, thinking it best to learn by experience rather than to be continually revealing my lamentable ignorance. If tarel were as scarce as his statement suggested, I should not have much picking to do, and that suited me perfectly. I am not lazy, but I like work that keeps my mind on the alert.

When we were both ready, Kamlot led the way upstairs, a procedure which mystified me, but did not tempt me into asking any more questions. We passed the two upper levels of the house and entered a dark, spiral staircase that led still farther upward into the tree. We ascended this for about fifteen feet, when Kamlot halted and I heard him fumbling with something above me.

Presently the shaft was bathed with light, which I saw came through a small circular opening that had been closed with a stout door. Through this opening Kamlot crawled, and I followed him, to find myself on a limb of the tree. My companion closed and locked the door, using a small key. I now saw that the door was covered on the outside with bark, so that when it was closed it would have been difficult for anyone to have detected it.

With almost monkeylike agility, Kamlot ascended, while I, resembling anything but a monkey in this respect, followed, thankful for the lesser gravitational pull of Venus, however little less than that of earth it might be, for I am not naturally arboreal.

After ascending about a hundred feet, Kamlot crossed to an adjacent tree, the branches of which interlocked with those of the one we had been ascending, and again the upward climb commenced. Occasionally the Vepajan stopped to listen as we passed from tree to tree or clambered to higher levels. After we had travelled for an hour or more, he stopped again and waited until I had overtaken him. A finger on his lips enjoined me to silence.

"Tarel," he whispered, pointing through the foliage in the direction of an adjacent tree.

I wondered why he had to whisper it, as my eyes followed the direction of his index finger. Twenty feet away I saw what appeared to be a huge spider web, partially concealed by the intervening foliage.

"Be ready with your spear," whispered Kamlot. "Put your hand through the loop. Follow me, but not too closely; you may need room to cast your spear. Do you see him?"

"No," I admitted. I saw nothing but the suggestion of a spider web; what else I was supposed to see I did not know.

"Neither do I, but he may be hiding. Look up occasionally so that he can't take you by surprise from above."

This was more exciting than picking cotton in Imperial Valley, though as yet I did not know just what there was to be excited about. Kamlot did not appear excited; he was very cool, but he was cautious. Slowly he crept toward the great web, his javelin ready in his hand; and I followed. When we were in full sight of it we saw that it was empty. Kamlot drew his dagger.

"Start cutting it away," he said. "Cut close to the branches and follow the web around; I will cut in the other direction until we meet. Be careful that you do not get enmeshed in it, especially if he happens to return."

"Can't we go around it?" I asked.

Kamlot looked puzzled. "Why should we go around it?" he demanded, a little shortly I thought.

"To get the tarel," I replied.

"What do you suppose this is?" he demanded.

"A spider's web."

"It is tarel."

I subsided. I had thought that the tarel he pointed at was beyond the web, although I had seen nothing; but then of course I had not known what tarel was or what it looked like. We had been cutting away for a few minutes when I heard a noise in a tree near us. Kamlot heard it at the same time.

"He is coming," he said. "Be ready!" He slipped his dagger into its sheath and grasped his spear. I followed his example.

The sound stopped, but I could see nothing through the foliage. Presently there was a rustling among the foliage, and a face appeared some fifteen yards from us. It was a hideous face—the face of a spider tremendously enlarged. When the thing saw that we had discovered it, it emitted the most frightful scream I had ever heard save once before. Then I recognized them—the voice and the face. It had been a creature such as this that had pursued my pursuer the night that I had dropped to the causeway in front of the house of Duran.

"Be ready," cautioned Kamlot; "he will charge."

The words had scarcely crossed the lips of the Vepajan when the hideous creature rushed toward us. Its body and legs were covered with long, black hair, and there was a yellow spot the size of a saucer above each eye. It screamed horribly as it came, as though to paralyze us with terror.

Kamlot's spear hand flew back and forward, and the heavy javelin, rushing to meet the maddened creature, buried itself deeply in the repulsive carcass; but it did not stop the charge. The creature was making straight for Kamlot as I hurled my javelin, which struck it in the side; but even this did not stop it, and to my horror I saw it seize my companion as he fell back upon the great limb upon which he had stood, with the spider on top of him.

The footing was secure enough for Kamlot and the spider, for they were both accustomed to it, but to me it seemed very precarious. Of course the tree limbs were enormous and often the branches were laced together, yet I felt anything but secure. However, I had no time to think of that now. If not already dead, Kamlot was being killed. Drawing my sword, I leaped to the side of the huge arachnid and struck viciously at its head, whereupon it abandoned Kamlot and turned upon me; but it was badly wounded now and moved with difficulty.

As I struck at that hideous face, I was horrified to see that Kamlot lay as though dead. He did not move. But I had only time for that single brief glance. If I were not careful I, too, should soon be dead. The thing confronting me seemed endowed with unsapable vitality. It was oozing sticky blood from several wounds, at least two of which I thought should have been almost instantly lethal; yet still it struggled to reach me with the powerful claws that terminated its forelegs, that it might draw me to those hideous jaws.

The Vepajan blade is a keen, two-edged affair, a little wider and thicker near the point than at the haft, and, while not well balanced to my way of thinking, is a deadly cutting weapon. I found it so in this my first experience with it, for as a great claw reached out to seize me I severed it with a single blow. At this the creature screamed more horribly

than ever, and with its last remaining vitality sprang upon me as you have seen spiders spring upon their prey. I cut at it again as I stepped back; and then thrust my point directly into that hideous visage, as the weight of the creature overbore me and I went down beneath it.

As it crashed upon me, my body toppled from the great branch upon which I had been standing, and I felt myself falling. Fortunately, the interlacing, smaller branches gave me some support; I caught at them and checked my fall, bringing up upon a broad, flat limb ten or fifteen feet below. I had clung to my sword, and being unhurt, clambered back as quickly as I could to save Kamlot from further attack, but he needed no protection—the great targo, as the creature is called, was dead.

Dead also was Kamlot; I could find no pulse nor detect any beating of the heart. My own sank within my breast. I had lost a friend, I who had so few here, and I was as utterly lost as one may be. I knew that I could not retrace our steps to the Vepajan city, even though my life depended upon my ability to do so, as it doubtless did. I could descend, but whether I was still over the city or not I did not know; I doubted it.

So this was gathering tarel; this was the occupation that I had feared would bore me with its monotony!

CHAPTER SEVEN

By Kamlot's Grave

Having set out to gather tarel, I finished the work that Kamlot and I had nearly completed when the targo attacked us; if I succeeded in finding the city, I should at least bring something to show for our efforts. But what about Kamlot? The idea of leaving the body here was repugnant to me. Even in the brief association I had had with the man I had come to like him and to look upon him as my friend. His people had befriended me; the least that I could do would be to take his body back to them. I realized, of course, that that was going to be something of a job, but it must be done. Fortunately, I am extraordinarily muscular, and then, too, the gravitational pull of Venus favored me more than would that of earth, giving me an advantage of over twenty pounds in the dead weight I should have to carry and even a little better than that in the amount of my own live weight, for I am heavier than Kamlot.

With less difficulty than I had anticipated I succeeded in getting Kamlot's body onto my back and trussed there with the cord attached to his javelin. I had previously strapped his weapons to him with strands of the tarel that half filled my bag, for, being unfamiliar with all the customs of the country, I did not know precisely what would be expected of me in an emergency of this nature, and preferred to be on the safe side.

The experiences of the next ten or twelve hours are a nightmare that I should like to forget. Contact with the dead and naked body of my companion was sufficiently gruesome, but the sense of utter bewilderment and futility in this strange world was even more depressing. As the hours passed, during which I constantly descended, except for brief rests, the weight of the corpse seemed to increase. In life Kamlot would have weighed about one hundred eighty pounds on earth, nearly one hundred sixty on Venus, but by the time darkness enveloped the gloomy forest I could have sworn that he weighed a ton.

So fatigued was I that I had to move very slowly, testing each new hand- and foothold before trusting my tired muscles to support the burden they were carrying, for a weak hold or a misstep would have plunged me into eternity. Death was ever at my elbow.

It seemed to me that I descended thousands of feet and yet I had seen no sign of the city. Several times I heard creatures moving through the trees at a distance, and twice I heard the hideous scream of a targo. Should one of these monstrous spiders attack me—well, I tried not to think about that. Instead I tried to occupy my mind with recollections of my earthly friends; I visualized my childhood days in India as I studied under old Chand Kabi, I thought of dear old Jimmy Welsh, and I recalled a bevy of girls I had liked and with some of whom I had almost been serious. These recalled the gorgeous girl in the garden of the jong, and the visions of the others faded into oblivion. Who was she? What strange interdiction had forbidden her to see or to speak with me? She had said that she loathed me, but she had heard me tell her that I loved her. That sounded rather silly now that I gave it thought. How could I love a girl the first instant that I laid eyes upon her, a girl concerning whom I knew absolutely nothing, neither her age nor her name? It was preposterous, yet I knew that it was true. I loved the nameless beauty of the little garden.

Perhaps my preoccupation with these thoughts made me careless; I do not know, but my mind was filled with them when my foot slipped a little after night had fallen. I grasped for support, but the combined weights of myself and the corpse tore my hands loose, and with my dead companion I plunged downward into the darkness. I felt Death's cold breath upon my cheek.

We did not fall far, being brought up suddenly by something soft that gave to our combined weights, then bounced up again, vibrating like a safety net such as we have all seen used by aerial performers. In the faint but all pervading light of the Amtorian night I could see what I had already guessed—I had fallen into the web of one of Amtor's ferocious spiders!

I tried to crawl to an edge where I might seize hold of a branch and drag myself free, but each move but entangled me the more. The situation was horrible enough, but a moment later it became infinitely worse, as, glancing about me, I saw at the far edge of the web the huge, repulsive body of a targo.

I drew my sword and hacked at the entangling meshes of the web as the fierce arachnid crept slowly toward me. I recall wondering if a fly entangled in a spider's web suffered the hopelessness and the mental anguish that seized me as I realized the futility of my puny efforts to escape this lethal trap and the ferocious monster advancing to devour me. But at least I had some advantages that no fly enjoys. I had my sword and a reasoning brain; I was not so entirely helpless as the poor fly.

The targo crept closer and closer. It uttered no sound. I presume that it was satisfied that I could not escape and saw no reason why it should seek to paralyze me with fright. From a distance of about ten feet it charged, moving with incredible swiftness upon its eight hairy legs. I met it with the point of my sword.

There was no skill in my thrust; it was just pure luck that my point penetrated the creature's tiny brain. When it collapsed lifeless beside me, I could scarcely believe the testimony of my eyes. I was saved!

Instantly I fell to work severing the strands of tarel that enmeshed me, and in four or five minutes I was free and had lowered myself to a branch below. My heart was still pounding rapidly and I was weak from exhaustion. For a quarter of an hour I remained resting; then I continued the seemingly endless descent out of this hideous forest.

What other dangers confronted me I could not guess. I knew that there were other creatures in this gigantic wood; those powerful webs, capable of sustaining the weight of an ox, had not been built for man alone. During the preceding day I had caught occasional glimpses of huge birds, which might themselves, if carnivorous, prove as deadly menaces as the targo; but it was not them that I feared now, but the nocturnal prowlers that haunt every forest by night.

Down and down I descended, feeling that each next moment must witness the final collapse of my endurance. The encounter with the targo had taken terrific toll of my great strength, already sapped by the arduous experiences of the day, yet I could not stop, I dared not. Yet how much longer could I drive exhausted nature on toward the brink of utter collapse?

I had about reached the end of my endurance when my feet struck solid ground. At first I could not believe the truth, but glancing down and about me I saw that I had indeed reached the floor of the forest; after a month on Venus I had at last placed foot upon her surface. I could see little or nothing—just the enormous boles of great trees in whatever direction I looked. Beneath my feet lay a thick matting of fallen leaves, turned white in death.

I cut the cords that bound the corpse of Kamlot to my back and lowered my poor comrade to the ground; then I threw myself down beside him and was asleep almost immediately.

When I awoke, it was daylight again. I looked about me, but could see nothing but the counterpane of whitened leaves spread between the boles of trees of such gargantuan girth that I almost hesitate to suggest the size of some of them, lest I discredit the veracity of this entire story of my experiences on Venus. But indeed they must needs be huge to support their extraordinary height, for many of them towered over six thousand feet above the surface of the ground, their lofty pinnacles enshrouded forever in the eternal fog of the inner cloud envelope.

To suggest an idea of the size of some of these monsters of the forest, I may say that I walked around the bole of one, counting over a thousand paces in the circuit, which gives, roughly, a diameter of a thousand feet, and there were many such. A tree ten feet in diameter appeared a frail and slender sapling—and there can be no vegetation upon Venus!

What little knowledge of physics I had and a very slight acquaintance with botany argued that trees of such height could not exist, but there must be some special, adaptive forces operating on Venus that permit the seemingly impossible. I have attempted to figure it out in terms of earthly conditions, and I have arrived at some conclusions that suggest possible explanations for the phenomenon. If vertical osmosis is affected by gravity, then the lesser gravity of Venus would favor the growth of taller trees, and the fact that their tops are forever in the clouds would permit them to build up an ample supply of carbohydrates from the abundant water vapor, provided there was the requisite amount of carbon dioxide in the atmosphere of Venus to promote this photosynthetic process.

I must admit, however, that at the time I was not greatly interested in these intriguing speculations; I had to think about myself and poor Kamlot. What was I to do with the corpse of my friend? I had done my best to return him to his people, and failed. I doubted now that I could ever find his people. There remained but a single alternative; I must bury him.

This decided, I started to scrape away the leaves beside him, that I might reach the ground beneath and dig a grave. There were about a foot of leaves and leaf mold and below that a soft, rich soil which I loosened easily with the point of my spear and scooped out with my hands. It did not take me long to excavate a nice grave; it was six feet long, two feet wide, and three feet deep. I gathered some freshly fallen leaves and carpeted its bottom with them, and then I gathered some more to place around and over Kamlot after I had lowered him to his final resting place.

While I worked I tried to recall the service for the dead; I wanted Kamlot to have as decent and orderly a burial as I could contrive. I wondered what God would think about it, but I had no doubt but that he would receive this first Amtorian soul to be launched into the unknown with a Christian burial and welcome him with open arms.

As I stooped and put my arms about the corpse to lower it into the grave, I was astounded to discover that it was quite warm. This put an entirely new aspect on the matter. A man dead for eighteen hours should be cold. Could it be that Kamlot was not dead? I pressed an ear to his chest; faintly I heard the beating of his heart. Never before had I experienced such an access of relief and joy. I felt as one reborn to new youth, to new hopes, to new aspirations. I had not realized until that instant the depth of my loneliness.

But why was Kamlot not dead? and how was I to resuscitate him? I felt that I should understand the former before I attempted the latter. I examined the wound again. There were two deep gashes on his chest just below the presternum. They had bled but little, and they were discolored, as I now noticed, by a greenish tint. It was this, meaningless though it may be, that suggested an explanation of Kamlot's condition. Something about that greenish tint suggested poison to my mind, and at once I recalled that there were varieties of spiders that paralyzed their victims by injecting a poison into them that preserved them in a state of suspended animation until they were ready to devour them. The targo had paralyzed Kamlot!

My first thought was to stimulate circulation and respiration, and to this end I alternately massaged his body and applied the first aid measures adapted to the resuscitation of the drowned. Which of these accomplished the result I do not know (perhaps each helped a little), but at any rate I was rewarded after a long period of effort with evidences of returning animation. Kamlot sighed and his eyelids fluttered. After another considerable period, during which I nearly exhausted myself, he opened his eyes and looked at me.

At first his gaze was expressionless and I thought that perhaps his mind had been affected by the poison; then a puzzled, questioning look entered his eyes and eventually recognition. I was witnessing a resurrection.

"What happened?" he asked in a whisper, and then, "Oh, yes, I recall; the targo got me." He sat up, with my assistance, and looked around. "Where are we?" he demanded.

"On the ground," I replied, "but where on the ground I do not know."

"You saved me from the targo," he said. "Did you kill it? But you must have, or you never could have gotten me away from it. Tell me about it."

Briefly, I told him. "I tried to get you back to the city, but I became lost and missed it. I have no idea where it lies."

"What is this?" he asked, glancing at the excavation beside him.

"Your grave," I replied. "I thought that you were dead."

"And you carried a corpse half a day and half a night! But why?"

"I do not know all the customs of your people," I replied; "but your family has been kind to me, and the least that I could do was to bring your body back to them, nor could I leave a friend up there to be devoured by birds and beasts."

"I shall not forget," he said quietly. He tried to rise then, but I had to assist him. "I shall be all right presently," he assured me, "after I have exercised a little. The effects of the targo's poison wear off in about twenty-four hours even without treatment. What you have done for me has helped to dissipate them sooner, and a little exercise will quickly eradicate the last vestiges of them." He stood looking about as though in an effort to orient himself, and as he did so his eyes fell upon his weapons, which I had intended burying with him and which lay on the ground beside the grave. "You even brought these!" he exclaimed. "You are a jong among friends!"

After he had buckled his sword belt about his hips, he picked up his spear, and together we walked through the forest, searching for some sign that would indicate that we had reached a point beneath the city, Kamlot having explained that trees along the important trails leading to the location of the city were marked in an inconspicuous and secret manner, as were certain trees leading upward to the hanging city.

"We come to the surface of Amtor but seldom," he said, "though occasionally trading parties descend and go to the coast to meet vessels from the few nations with which we carry on a surreptitious commerce. The curse of Thorism has spread far, however, and there are few nations of which we have knowledge that are not subject to its cruel and selfish domination. Once in a while we descend to hunt the basto for its hide and flesh."

"What is a basto?" I inquired.

"It is a large, omnivorous animal with powerful jaws armed with four great fangs in addition to its other teeth. On its head grow two heavy horns. At the shoulder it is as tall as a tall man. I have killed them that weighed thirty-six hundred tob."

A tob is the Amtorian unit of weight, and is the equivalent of one third of an English pound; all weights are computed in tobs or decimals thereof, as they use the decimal system exclusively in their tables of weights and measures. It seems to me much more practical than the confusing earthly collection of grains, grams, ounces, pounds, tons, and the other designations in common use among the various nations of our planet.

From Kamlot's description I visualized the basto as an enormous boar with horns, or a buffalo with the jaws and teeth of a carnivore, and judged that its twelve hundred pounds of weight would render it a most formidable beast. I asked him with what weapons they hunted the animal.

"Some prefer arrows, others spears," he explained, "and it is always handy to have a low branched tree near by," he added with a grin.

"They are bellicose?" I asked.

"Very. When a basto appears upon the scene, man is as often the hunted as the hunter, but we are not hunting bastos now. What I should most like to find is a sign that would tell me where we are."

We moved on through the forest, searching for the tiny road signs of the Vepajans, which Kamlot had described to me as well as explaining the location in which they are always placed. The sign consists of a long, sharp nail with a flat head bearing a number in relief. These nails are driven into trees at a uniform height from the ground. They are difficult to find, but it is necessary to have them so, lest the enemies of the Vepajans find and remove them, or utilize them in their search for the cities of the latter.

The method of the application of these signs to the requirements of the Vepajans is clever. They would really be of little value to any but a Vepajan as guide posts, yet each nail tells a remarkable story to the initiated; briefly it tells him precisely where he is on the island that comprises the kingdom of Mintep, the jong. Each nail is placed in position by a surveying party and its exact location is indicated on a map of the island, together with the number on the head of the nail. Before a Vepajan is permitted to descend to the ground alone, or to lead others there, he must memorize the location of every sign nail in Vepaja. Kamlot had done so. He told me that if we could find but a single nail he would immediately know the direction of and distance to those on either side of it, our exact position upon the island, and the location of the city; but he admitted that we might wander a long time before we discovered a single nail.

The forest was monotonously changeless. There were trees of several species, some with branches that trailed the ground, others bare of branches for hundreds of feet from their bases. There were boles as smooth as glass and as straight as a ship's mast, without a single branch as far up as the eye could see. Kamlot told me that the foliage of these grew in a single enormous tuft far up among the clouds.

I asked him if he had ever been up there, and he said he had climbed, he believed, to the top of the tallest tree, but that he had nearly frozen to death in the attempt. "We get our water supply from these trees," he remarked. "They drink in the water vapor among the clouds and carry it down to their roots. They are unlike any other tree. A central, porous core carries the water from the clouds to the roots, from whence it rises again in the form of sap that carries the tree's food upward from the ground. By tapping one of these trees anywhere you may obtain a copious supply of clear, cool water—a fortunate provision of——"

"Something is coming, Kamlot," I interrupted. "Do you hear it?"

He listened intently for a moment. "Yes," he replied. "We had better take to a tree, at least until we see what it is."

As he climbed into the branches of a near-by tree, I followed him; and there we waited. Distinctly I could hear something moving through the forest as it approached us. The soft carpet of leaves beneath its feet gave forth but little sound—just a rustling of the dry leaves. Nearer and nearer it came, apparently moving leisurely; then, suddenly, its great head came into view from behind the bole of a tree a short distance from us.

"A basto," whispered Kamlot, but from his previous description of the beast I had already guessed its identity.

It looked like a basto, only more so. From the eyes up its head resembled that of an American bison, with the same short, powerful horns. Its poll and forehead were covered with thick, curly hair, its eyes were small and red-rimmed. Its hide was blue and of about the same texture as that of an elephant, with sparsely growing hairs except upon the head and at the tip of the tail. It stood highest at the shoulders and sloped rapidly to its rump. Its front legs were short and stocky and ended in broad, three-toed feet; its hind legs were longer and the hind feet smaller, a difference necessitated by the fact that the forelegs and feet carried fully three quarters of the beast's weight. Its muzzle was similar to that of a boar, except that it was broader, and carried heavy, curved tusks.

"Here comes our next meal," remarked Kamlot in an ordinary tone of voice. The basto stopped and looked about as he heard my companion's voice. "They are mighty good eating," added Kamlot, "and we have not eaten for a long while. There is nothing like a basto steak grilled over a wood fire."

My mouth commenced to water. "Come on," I said, and started to climb down from the tree, my spear ready in my hand.

"Come back!" called Kamlot. "You don't know what you are doing."

The basto had located us and was advancing, uttering a sound that would have put to shame the best efforts of a full-grown lion. I do not know whether to describe it as a bellow or a roar. It started with a series of grunts and then rose in volume until it shook the ground.

"He seems to be angry," I remarked; "but if we are going to eat him we must kill him first, and how are we to kill him if we remain in the tree?"

"I am not going to remain in the tree," replied Kamlot, "but you are. You know nothing about hunting these beasts, and you would probably not only get yourself killed but me into the bargain. You stay where you are. I will attend to the basto."

This plan did not suit me at all, but I was forced to admit Kamlot's superior knowledge of things Amtorian and his greater experience and defer to his wishes; but nevertheless I held myself ready to go to his assistance should occasion require.

To my surprise, he dropped his spear to the ground and carried in its stead a slender leafy branch which he cut from the tree before descending to engage the bellowing basto. He did not come down to the floor of the forest directly in front of the beast, but made his way part way around the tree before descending, after asking me to keep the basto's attention diverted, which I did by shouting and shaking a branch of the tree.

Presently, to my horror, I saw Kamlot out in the open a dozen paces in rear of the animal, armed only with his sword and the leafy branch which he carried in his left hand. His spear lay on the ground not far from the enraged beast and his position appeared utterly hopeless should the basto discover him before he could reach the safety of another tree. Realizing this, I redoubled my efforts to engage the creature's attention, until Kamlot shouted to me to desist.

I thought that he must have gone crazy and should not have heeded him had not his voice attracted the attention of the basto and frustrated any attempt that I might have made to keep the beast's eyes upon me. The instant that Kamlot called to me the great head turned ponderously in his direction and the savage eyes discovered him. The creature wheeled and stood for a moment eyeing the rash but puny man-thing; then it trotted toward him.

I waited no longer but dropped to the ground with the intention of attacking the thing from the rear. What happened thereafter happened so quickly that it was over almost in the time it takes to tell it. As I started in pursuit, I saw the mighty basto lower its head and charge straight for my companion, who stood there motionless with his puny sword and the leafy branch grasped one in either hand. Suddenly, at the very instant that I thought the creature was about to impale him on those mighty horns, he waved the leaf covered branch in its face and leaped lightly to one side, simultaneously driving the keen point of his blade downward from a point in front of the left shoulder until the steel was buried to the hilt in the great carcass.

The basto stopped, its four legs spread wide; for an instant it swayed, and then it crashed to the ground at the feet of Kamlot. A shout of admiration was on my lips when I chanced to glance upward. What attracted my attention I do not know, perhaps the warning of that inaudible voice which we sometimes call a sixth sense. What I saw drove the basto and the feat of Kamlot from my thoughts.

"My God!" I cried in English, and then in Amtorian, "Look, Kamlot! What are those?"

CHAPTER EIGHT

On Board the Sofal

Hovering just above us, I saw what at first appeared to be five enormous birds, but which I soon recognized, despite my incredulity, as winged men. They were armed with swords and daggers, and each carried a long rope at the end of which dangled a wire noose.

"Voo klangan!" shouted Kamlot. (The birdmen!)

Even as he spoke a couple of wire nooses settled around each of us. We struggled to free ourselves, striking at the snares with our swords, but our blades made no impression upon the wires, and the ropes to which they were attached were beyond our reach. As we battled futilely to disengage ourselves, the klangan settled to the ground, each pair upon opposite sides of the victim they had snared. Thus they held us so that we were helpless, as two cowboys hold a roped steer, while the fifth angan approached us with drawn sword and disarmed us. (Perhaps I should explain that angan is singular, klangan plural, plurals of Amtorian words being formed by prefixing kloo to words commencing with a consonant and kl to those commencing with a vowel.)

Our capture had been accomplished so quickly and so deftly that it was over, with little or no effort on the part of the birdmen, before I had had time to recover from the astonishment that their weird appearance induced. I now recalled having heard Danus speak of *voo klangan* upon one or two occasions, but I had thought that he referred to poultry breeders or something of that sort. How little could I have dreamed of the reality!

"I guess we are in for it," remarked Kamlot gloomily.

"What will they do with us?" I inquired.

"Ask them," he replied.

"Who are you?" demanded one of our captors.

For some reason I was astonished to hear him speak, although I do not know why anything should have astonished me now. "I am a stranger from another world," I told him. "My friend and I have no quarrel with you. Let us go."

"You are wasting your breath," Kamlot advised me.

"Yes, he is wasting his breath," agreed the angan. "You are Vepajans, and we have orders to bring Vepajans to the ship. You do not look like a Vepajan," he added, surveying me from head to feet, "but the other does."

"Anyway, you are not a Thorist, and therefore you must be an enemy," interjected another.

They removed the nooses from about us and tied ropes around our necks and other ropes about our bodies beneath our arms; then two klangan seized the ropes attached to Kamlot and two more those attached to me, and, spreading their wings, rose into the air, carrying us with them. Our weight was supported by the ropes beneath our arms, but the other ropes were a constant suggestion to us of what might happen if we did not behave ourselves.

As they flew, winding their way among the trees, our bodies were suspended but a few feet above the ground, for the forest lanes were often low ceiled by overhanging branches. The klangan talked a great deal among themselves, shouting to one another and laughing and singing, seemingly well satisfied with themselves and their exploit. Their voices were soft and mellow, and their songs were vaguely reminiscent of Negro spirituals, a similarity which may have been enhanced by the color of their skins, which were very dark.

As Kamlot was carried in front of me, I had an opportunity to observe the physical characteristics of these strange creatures into whose hands we had fallen. They had low, receding foreheads, huge, beaklike noses, and undershot jaws; their eyes were small and close set, their ears flat and slightly pointed. Their chests were large and shaped like those of birds, and their arms were very long, ending in long-fingered, heavy-nailed hands. The lower part of the torso was small, the hips narrow, the legs very short and stocky, ending in three-toed feet equipped with long, curved talons. Feathers grew upon their heads instead of hair. When they were excited, as when they attacked us, these feathers stand erect, but ordinarily they lie flat. They are all alike; commencing near the root they are marked with a band of white, next comes a band of black, then another of white, and the tip is red. Similar feathers also grow at the lower extremity of the torso in front, and there is another, quite large bunch just above the buttocks—a gorgeous tail which they open into a huge pompon when they wish to show off.

Their wings, which consist of a very thin membrane supported on a light framework, are similar in shape to those of a bat and do not appear adequate to the support of the apparent weight of the creatures' bodies, but I was to learn later that this apparent weight is deceptive, since their bones, like the bones of true birds, are hollow.

The creatures carried us a considerable distance, though how far I do not know. We were in the air fully eight hours; and, where the forest permitted, they flew quite rapidly. They seemed utterly tireless, though Kamlot and I were all but exhausted long before they reached their destination. The ropes beneath our arms cut into our flesh, and this contributed to our exhaustion as did our efforts to relieve the agony by seizing the ropes above us and supporting the weight of our bodies with our hands.

But, as all things must, this hideous journey ended at last. Suddenly we broke from the forest and winged out across a magnificent land-locked harbor, and for the first time I looked upon the waters of a Venusan sea. Between two points that formed the harbor's entrance I could see it stretching away as far as the eye could reach—mysterious, intriguing, provocative. What strange lands and stranger people lay off there beyond the beyond? Would I ever know?

Suddenly now my attention and my thoughts were attracted to something in the left foreground that I had not before noticed; a ship lay at anchor on the quiet waters of the harbor and just beyond it a second ship. Toward one of them our captors were winging. As we approached the nearer and smaller, I saw a craft that differed but little in the lines of its hull from earthly ships. It had a very high bow, its prow was sharp and sloped forward in a scimitarlike curve; the ship was long and narrow of beam. It looked as though it might have been built for speed. But what was its motive power? It had no masts, sails, stacks, nor funnels. Aft were two oval houses—a smaller one resting upon the top of a larger; on top of the upper house was an oval tower surmounted by a small crow's nest. There were doors and windows in the two houses and the tower. As we came closer, I could see a number of open hatches in the deck and people standing on the walkways that surrounded the tower and the upper house and also upon the main deck. They were watching our approach.

As our captors deposited us upon the deck, we were immediately surrounded by a horde of jabbering men. A man whom I took to be an officer ordered the ropes removed from us, and while this was being done he questioned the klangan who had brought us.

All the men that I saw were similar in color and physique to the Vepajans, but their countenances were heavy and unintelligent; very few of them were good-looking, and only one or two might have been called handsome. I saw evidences of age among them and of disease—the first I had seen on Amtor.

After the ropes had been removed, the officer ordered us to follow him, after detailing four villainous-looking fellows to guard us, and conducted us aft and up to the tower that surmounted the smaller house. Here he left us outside the tower, which he entered.

The four men guarding us eyed us with surly disfavor. "Vepajans, eh!" sneered one. "Think you're better than ordinary men, don't you? But you'll find out you ain't, not in The Free Land of Thora; there everybody's equal. I don't see no good in bringing your kind into the country anyway. If I had my way you'd get a dose of this," and he tapped a weapon that hung in a holster at his belt.

The weapon, or the grip of it, suggested a pistol of some kind, and I supposed that it was one of those curious firearms discharging deadly rays, that Kamlot had described to me. I was about to ask the fellow to let me see it when the officer emerged from the tower and ordered the guard to bring us in.

We were escorted into a room in which sat a scowling man with a most unprepossessing countenance. There was a sneer on his face as he appraised us, the sneer of the inferior man for his superior, that tries to hide but only reveals the inferiority complex that prompts it. I knew that I was not going to like him.

"Two more klooganfal!" he exclaimed. (A ganfal is a criminal.) "Two more of the beasts that tried to grind down the workers; but you didn't succeed, did you? Now we are the masters. You'll find that out even before we reach Thora. Is either of you a doctor?"

Kamlot shook his head. "Not I," he said.

The fellow, whom I took to be the captain of the ship, eyed me closely. "You are no Vepajan," he said. "What are you, anyway? No one ever saw a man with yellow hair and blue eyes before."

"As far as you are concerned," I replied, "I am a Vepajan. I have never been in any other country in Amtor."

"What do you mean by saying as far as I am concerned?" he demanded.

"Because it doesn't make any difference what you think about it," I snapped. I did not like the fellow, and when I do not like people I have difficulty in hiding the fact. In this case I did not try to hide it.

He flushed and half rose from his chair. "It doesn't, eh?" he cried.

"Sit down," I advised him. "You're here under orders to bring back Vepajans. Nobody cares what you think about them, but you'll get into trouble if you don't bring them back."

Diplomacy would have curbed my tongue, but I am not particularly diplomatic, especially when I am angry, and now I was both angry and disgusted, for there had been something in the attitude of all these people toward us that bespoke ignorant prejudice and bitterness. Furthermore, I surmised from scraps of information I had picked up from Danus, as well as from the remarks of the sailor who had announced that he would like to kill us, that I was not far wrong in my assumption that the officer I had thus addressed would be exceeding his authority if he harmed us. However, I realized that I was taking chances, and awaited with interest the effect of my words.

The fellow took them like a whipped cur and subsided after a single weakly blustering, "We'll see about that." He turned to a book that lay open before him. "What is your name?" he asked, nodding in Kamlot's direction. Even his nod was obnoxious.

"Kamlot of Zar," replied my companion.

"What is your profession?"

"Hunter and wood carver."

"You are a Vepajan?"

"Yes."

"From what city of Vepaja?"

"From Kooaad," replied Kamlot.

"And you?" demanded the officer, addressing me.

"I am Carson of Napier," I replied, using the Amtorian form; "I am a Vepajan from Kooaad."

"What is your profession?"

"I am an *aviator,*" I replied, using the English word and English pronunciation.

"A what?" he demanded. "I never heard of such a thing." He tried to write the word in his book and then he tried to pronounce it, but he could do neither, as the Amtorians have no equivalents for many of our vowel sounds and seem unable even to pronounce them. Had I written the word for him in Amtorian he would have pronounced it ah-vy-ah-tore, as they cannot form the long *a* and short *o* sounds, and their *i* is always long.

Finally, to cover his ignorance, he wrote something in his book, but what it was I did not know; then he looked up at me again. "Are you a doctor?"

"Yes," I replied, and as the officer made the notation in his book, I glanced at Kamlot out of the corner of an eye and winked.

"Take them away," the man now directed, "and be careful of this one," he added, indicating me; "he is a doctor."

We were taken to the main deck and led forward to the accompaniment of jeers and jibes from the sailors congregated on the deck. I saw the klangan strutting around, their tail feathers erect. When they saw us, they pointed at Kamlot, and I heard them telling some of the sailors that he was the one who had slain the basto with a single sword thrust, a feat which appeared to force their admiration, as well it might have.

We were escorted to an open hatch and ordered below into a dark, poorly ventilated hole, where we found several other prisoners. Some of them were Thorans undergoing punishment for infractions of discipline; others were Vepajan captives like ourselves, and among the latter was one who recognized Kamlot and hailed him as we descended into their midst.

"Jodades, Kamlot!" he cried, voicing the Amtorian greeting "luck-to-you."

"Ra jodades," replied Kamlot; "what ill fortune brings Honan here?"

" 'Ill fortune' does not describe it," replied Honan; "catastrophe would be a better word. The klangan were seeking women as well as men; they saw Duare" (pronounced Doo-ah'-ree) "and pursued her; as I sought to protect her they captured me."

"Your sacrifice was not in vain," said Kamlot; "had you died in the performance of such a duty it would not have been in vain."

"But it was in vain; that is the catastrophe."

"What do you mean?" demanded Kamlot.

"I mean that they got her," replied Honan dejectedly.

"They captured Duare!" exclaimed Kamlot in tones of horror. "By the life of the jong, it cannot be."

"I wish it were not," said Honan.

"Where is she? on this ship?" demanded Kamlot.

"No; they took her to the other, the larger one."

Kamlot appeared crushed, and I could only attribute his dejection to the hopelessness of a lover who has irretrievably lost his beloved. Our association had not been either sufficiently close nor long to promote confidences, and so I was not surprised that I had never heard him mention the girl, Duare, and, naturally, under the circumstances, I could not question him concerning her. I therefore respected his grief and his silence, and left him to his own sad thoughts.

Shortly after dawn the following morning the ship got under way. I wished that I might have been on deck to view the fascinating sights of this strange world, and my precarious situation as a prisoner of the hated Thorists engendered less regret than the fact that I, the first earth man to sail the seas of Venus, was doomed to be cooped up in a stuffy hole below deck where I could see nothing. But if I had feared being kept below for the duration of the voyage, I was soon disillusioned, for shortly after the ship got under way we were all ordered on deck and set to scrubbing and polishing.

As we came up from below, the ship was just passing between the two headlands that formed the entrance to the harbor, in the wake of the larger vessel; and I obtained an excellent view of the adjacent land, the shore that we were leaving, and the wide expanse of ocean stretching away to the horizon.

The headlands were rocky promontories clothed with verdure of delicate hues and supporting comparatively few trees, which were of a smaller variety than the giants upon the mainland. These latter presented a truly awe inspiring spectacle from the open sea to the eyes of an earth man, their mighty boles rearing their weirdly colored foliage straight up for five thousand feet, where they were lost to view among the clouds. But I was not permitted to gaze for long upon the wonders of the scene. I had not been ordered above for the purpose of satisfying the æsthetic longings of my soul.

Kamlot and I were set to cleaning and polishing guns. There were a number of these on either side of the deck, one at the stern, and two on the tower deck. I was surprised when I saw them, for there had been no sign of armament when I came on board the preceding day; but I was not long in discovering the explanation—the guns were mounted on disappearing carriages, and when lowered, a sliding hatch, flush with the deck, concealed them.

The barrels of these pieces were about eight inches in diameter, while the bore was scarcely larger than my little finger; the sights were ingenious and complicated, but there was no breech block in evidence nor any opening into a breech, unless there was one hidden beneath a hoop that encircled the breech, to which it was heavily bolted. The only thing that I could discover that might have been a firing device projected from the rear of the breech and resembled the rotating crank that is used to revolve the breech block in some types of earthly guns.

The barrels of the guns were about fifteen feet long and of the same diameter from breech to muzzle. When in action they can be extended beyond the rail of the ship about two thirds of their length, thus affording a wider horizontal range and more deck room, which would be of value on a ship such as that on which I was a captive, which was of narrow beam.

"What do these guns fire?" I asked Kamlot, who was working at my side.

"T-rays," he replied.

"Do those differ materially from the R-rays you described when you were telling me about the small arms used by the Thorans?"

"The R-ray destroys only animal tissue," he replied, "while there is nothing that the T-ray may not dissipate. It is a most dangerous ray to work with because even the material of the gun barrel itself is not wholly impervious to it, and the only reason that it can be used at all is that its greatest force is expended along the line of least resistance, which in this case naturally is the bore of the gun. But eventually it destroys the gun itself."

"How is it fired?" I asked.

He touched the crank at the end of the breech. "By turning this, a shutter is raised that permits radiations from element 93 to impinge on the charge, which consists of element 97, thus releasing the deadly T-ray."

"Why couldn't we turn this gun about and rake the ship above deck," I suggested, "thus wiping out the Thorans and giving us our freedom?"

He pointed to a small, irregular hole in the end of the crank shaft. "Because we haven't the key that fits this," he replied.

"Who has the key?"

"The officers have keys to the guns they command," he replied. "In the captain's cabin are keys to all the guns, and he carries a master key that will unlock any of them. At least that was the system in the ancient Vepajan navy, and it is doubtless the same today in the Thoran navy."

"I wish we could get hold of the master key," I said.

"So do I," he agreed, "but that is impossible."

"Nothing is impossible," I retorted.

He made no answer, and I did not pursue the subject, but I certainly gave it a lot of thought.

As I worked, I noted the easy, noiseless propulsion of the ship and asked Kamlot what drove it. His explanation was long and rather technical; suffice it to say that the very useful element 93 (vik-ro) is here again employed upon a substance called lor, which contains a considerable proportion of the element yor-san (105). The action of vik-ro upon yor-san results in absolute annihilation of the lor, releasing all its energy. When you consider that there is eighteen thousand million times as much energy liberated by the annihilation of a ton of coal than by its combustion you will appreciate the inherent possibilities of this marvellous Venusan scientific discovery. Fuel for the life of the ship could be carried in a pint jar.

I noticed as the day progressed that we cruised parallel to a coast line, after crossing one stretch of ocean where no land was in sight, and thereafter for several days I noted the same fact—land was almost always in sight. This suggested that the land area of Venus might be much greater in proportion to its seas; but I had no opportunity to satisfy my curiosity on that point, and of course I took no stock in the maps that Danus had shown me, since the Amtorians' conception of the shape of their world precluded the existence of any dependable maps.

Kamlot and I had been separated, he having been detailed to duty in the ship's galley, which was located in the forward part of the main deck house aft. I struck up a friendship with Honan; but we did not work together, and at night we were usually so tired that we conversed but little before falling asleep on the hard floor of our prison. One night, however, the sorrow of Kamlot having been brought to my mind by my own regretful recollections of the nameless girl of the garden, I asked Honan who Duare was.

"She is the hope of Vepaja," he replied, "perhaps the hope of a world."

CHAPTER NINE

Soldiers of Liberty

Constant association breeds a certain *camaraderie* even between enemies. As the days passed, the hatred and contempt which the common sailors appeared to have harbored for us when we first came aboard the ship were replaced by an almost friendly familiarity, as though they had discovered that we were not half bad fellows after all; and, for my part, I found much to like in these simple though ignorant men. That they were the dupes of unscrupulous leaders is about the worst that may be said of them. Most of them were kindly and generous; but their ignorance made them gullible, and their emotions were easily aroused by specious arguments that would have made no impression upon intelligent minds.

Naturally, I became better acquainted with my fellow prisoners than with my guards, and our relations were soon established upon a friendly basis. They were greatly impressed by my blond hair and blue eyes which elicited inquiries as to my genesis. As I answered their questions truthfully, they became deeply interested in my story, and every evening after the day's work was completed I was besieged for tales of the mysterious, far distant world from which I came. Unlike the highly intelligent Vepajans, they believed all that I told them, with the result that I was soon a hero in their eyes; I should have been a god had they had any conception of deities of any description.

In turn, I questioned them; and discovered, with no surprise, that they were not at all contented with their lots. The former free men among them had long since come to the realization that they had exchanged this freedom, and their status of wage earners, for slavery to the state, that could no longer be hidden by a nominal equality.

Among the prisoners were three to whom I was particularly attracted by certain individual characteristics in each. There was Gamfor, for instance, a huge, hulking fellow who had been a farmer in the old days under the jongs. He was unusually intelligent, and although he had taken part in the revolution, he was now bitter in his denunciation of the Thorists, though this he was careful to whisper to me in secrecy.

Another was Kiron, the soldier, a clean-limbed, handsome, athletic fellow who had served in the army of the jong, but mutinied with the others at the time of the revolution. He was being disciplined now for insubordination to an officer who had been a petty government clerk before his promotion.

The third had been a slave. His name was Zog. What he lacked in intelligence he made up in strength and good nature. He had killed an officer who had struck him and was being taken back to Thora for trial and execution. Zog was proud of the fact that he was a free man, though he admitted that the edge was taken off his enthusiasm by the fact that every one else was free and the realization that he had enjoyed more freedom as a slave than he did now as a freeman.

"Then," he explained, "I had one master; now I have as many masters as there are government officials, spies, and soldiers, none of whom cares anything about me, while my old master was kind to me and looked after my welfare."

"Would you like to be really free?" I asked him, for a plan had been slowly forming in my mind.

But to my surprise he said, "No, I should rather be a slave."

"But you'd like to choose your own master, wouldn't you?" I demanded.

"Certainly," he replied, "if I could find some one who would be kind to me and protect me from the Thorists."

"And if you could escape from them now, you would like to do so?"

"Of course! But what do you mean? I cannot escape from them."

"Not without help," I agreed, "but if others would join you, would you make the attempt?"

"Why not? They are taking me back to Thora to kill me. I could be no worse off, no matter what I did. But why do you ask all these questions?"

"If we could get enough to join us, there is no reason why we should not be free," I told him. "When you are free, you may remain free or choose a master to your liking." I watched closely for his reaction.

"You mean another revolution?" he asked. "It would fail. Others have tried, but they have always failed."

"Not a revolution," I assured him, "just a break for liberty."

"But how could we do it?"

"It would not be difficult for a few men to take this ship," I suggested. "The discipline is poor, the night watches consist of too few men; they are so sure of themselves that they would be taken completely by surprise."

Zog's eyes lighted. "If we were successful, many of the crew would join us," he said. "Few of them are happy; nearly all of them hate their officers. I think the prisoners would join us almost to a man, but you must be careful of spies—they are everywhere. That is the greatest danger you would have to face. There can be no doubt but there is at least one spy among us prisoners."

"How about Gamfor," I asked; "is he all right?"

"You can depend upon Gamfor," Zog assured me. "He does not say much, but in his eyes I can read his hatred of them."

"And Kiron?"

"Just the man!" exclaimed Zog. "He despises them, and he does not care who knows it; that is the reason he is a prisoner. This is not his first offense, and it is rumored that he will be executed for high treason."

"But I thought that he only talked back to an officer and refused to obey him," I said.

"That is high treason—if they wish to get rid of a man," explained Zog. "You can depend on Kiron. Do you wish me to speak to him about the matter?"

"No," I told him. "I will speak to him and to Gamfor; then if anything goes wrong before we are ready to strike, if a spy gets wind of our plot, you will not be implicated."

"I do not care about that;" he exclaimed. "They can kill me for but one thing, and it makes no difference which thing it is they kill me for."

"Nevertheless, I shall speak to them, and if they will join us, we can then decide together how to approach others."

Zog and I had been working together scrubbing the deck at the time, and it was not until night that I had an opportunity to speak with Gamfor and Kiron. Both were enthusiastic about the plan, but neither thought that there was much likelihood that it would succeed. However, each assured me of his support; and then we found Zog, and the four of us discussed details throughout half the night. We had withdrawn to a far corner of the room in which we were confined and spoke in low whispers with our heads close together.

The next few days were spent in approaching recruits—a very ticklish business, since they all assured me that it was almost a foregone conclusion that there was a spy among us. Each man had to be sounded out by devious means, and it had been decided that this work should be left to Gamfor and Kiron. I was eliminated because of my lack of knowledge concerning the hopes, ambitions, and the grievances of these people, or their psychology; Zog was eliminated because the work required a much higher standard of intelligence than he possessed.

Gamfor warned Kiron not to divulge our plan to any prisoner who too openly avowed his hatred of the Thorists. "This is a time-worn trick that all spies adopt to lull the suspicions of those they suspect of harboring treasonable thoughts, and to tempt them into avowing their apostasy. Select men whom you know to have a real grievance, and who are moody and silent," he counselled.

I was a little concerned about our ability to navigate the ship in the event that we succeeded in capturing her, and I discussed this matter with both Gamfor and Kiron. What I learned from them was illuminating, if not particularly helpful.

The Amtorians have developed a compass similar to ours. According to Kiron, it points always toward the center of Amtor—that is, toward the center of the mythical circular area called Strabol, or Hot Country. This statement assured me that I was in the southern hemisphere of the planet, the needle of the compass, of course, pointing north toward the north magnetic pole. Having no sun, moon, nor stars, their navigation is all done by dead reckoning; but they have developed instruments of extreme delicacy that locate land at great distances, accurately indicating this distance and the direction; others that determine speed, mileage, and drift, as well as a depth gauge wherewith they may record soundings anywhere within a radius of a mile from the ship.

All of their instruments for measuring distances utilize the radioactivity of the nuclei of various elements to accomplish their ends. The gamma ray, for which they have, of course, another name, being uninfluenced by the most powerful magnetic forces, is naturally the ideal medium for their purposes. It moves in a straight line and at uniform speed until it meets an obstruction, where, even though it may not be deflected, it is retarded, the instrument recording such retardation and the distance at which it occurs. The sounding device utilizes the same principle. The instrument records the distance from the ship at which the ray encounters the resistance of the ocean's bottom; by constructing a right triangle with this distance representing the hypotenuse it is simple to compute both the depth of the ocean and the distance from the ship at which bottom was found, for they have a triangle of which one side and all three angles are known.

Owing to their extremely faulty maps, however, the value of these instruments has been greatly reduced, for no matter what course they lay, other than due north, if they move in a straight line they are always approaching the antarctic regions. They may know that land is ahead and its distance, but they are never sure what land it is; except where the journey is a short and familiar one. For this reason they cruise within sight of land wherever that is practical, with the result that journeys that might otherwise be short are greatly protracted. Another result is that the radius of Amtorian maritime exploration has been greatly circumscribed; so much so that I believe there are enormous areas in the south temperate zone that have never been discovered by the Vepajans or the Thorists, while the very existence of the northern hemisphere is even unguessed by them. On the maps that Danus showed me considerable areas contained nothing but the single word *joram,* ocean.

However, notwithstanding all this (and possibly because of it), I was confident that we could manage to navigate the ship quite as satisfactorily as her present officers, and in this Kiron agreed.

"At least we know the general direction of Thora," he argued; "so all we have to do is sail in the other direction."

As our plans matured, the feasibility of the undertaking appeared more and more certain. We had recruited twenty prisoners, five of whom were Vepajans, and this little band we organized into a secret order with passwords, which were changed daily, signs, and a grip, the last reminiscent of my fraternity days in college. We also adopted a name. We called ourselves Soldiers of Liberty. I was chosen vookor, or captain. Gamfor, Kiron, Zog, and Honan were my principal lieutenants, though I told them that Kamlot would be second in command if we were successful in taking the ship.

Our plan of action was worked out in detail; each man knew exactly what was expected of him. Certain men were to overpower the watch, others were to go to the officers' quarters and secure their weapons and keys; then we would confront the crew and offer those who chose an opportunity to join us. The others—well, there I was confronted with a problem. Almost to a man the Soldiers of Liberty wanted to destroy all those who would not join us, and really there seemed no alternative; but I still hoped that I could work out a more humane disposition of them.

There was one man among the prisoners of whom we were all suspicious. He had an evil face, but that was not his sole claim upon our suspicions—he was too loud in his denunciation of Thorism. We watched him carefully, avoiding him whenever we could, and each member of the band was warned to be careful when talking to him. It was evident to Gamfor first that this fellow, whose name was Anoos, was suspicious. He persisted in seeking out various members of our group and engaging them in conversation which he always led around to the subject of Thorism and his hatred of it, and he constantly questioned each of us about the others, always insinuating that he feared certain ones were spies. But of course we had expected something of this sort, and we felt that we had guarded against it. The fellow might be as suspicious of us as he wished; so long as he had no evidence against us I did not see how he could harm us.

One day Kiron came to me evidently laboring under suppressed excitement. It was at the end of the day, and our food had just been issued to us for the evening meal—dried fish and a hard, dark-colored bread made of coarse meal.

"I have news, Carson," he whispered.

"Let us go off in a corner and eat," I suggested, and we strolled away together, laughing talking of the day's events in our normal voices. As we seated ourselves upon the floor to eat our poor food, Zog joined us.

"Sit close to us, Zog," directed Kiron; "I have something to say that no one but a Soldier of Liberty may hear."

He did not say Soldier of Liberty, but "kung, kung, kung," which are the Amtorian initials of the order's title. Kung is the name of the Amtorian character that represents the *k* sound in our language, and when I first translated the initials I was compelled to smile at the similarity they bore to those of a well-known secret order in the United States of America.

"While I am talking," Kiron admonished us, "you must laugh often, as though I were telling a humorous tale; then, perhaps, no one will suspect that I am not.

"Today I was working in the ship's armory, cleaning pistols," he commenced. "The soldier who guarded me is an old friend of mine; we served together in the army of the jong. He is as a brother to me. For either the other would die. We talked of old times under the banners of the jong and compared those days with these, especially we compared the officers of the old régime with those of the present. Like me and like every old soldier, he hates his officers; so we had a pleasant time together.

"Finally he said to me, quite suddenly, 'What is this I hear of a conspiracy among the prisoners?'

"That almost took me off my feet; but I showed no emotion, for there are times when one must not trust even a brother. 'What have you heard?' I asked.

" 'I overheard one of the officers speaking to another,' he told me. 'He said that a man named Anoos had reported the matter to the captain, and that the captain had told Anoos to get the names of all the prisoners whom he knew to be involved in the conspiracy and to learn their plans if he possibly could.'

" 'And what did Anoos say?' I asked my friend.

" 'He said that if the captain would give him a bottle of wine he believed that he could get one of the conspirators drunk and worm the story from him. So the captain gave him a bottle of wine. That was today.'

"My friend looked at me very closely, and then he said, 'Kiron, we are more than brothers. If I can help you, you have but to ask.'

"I knew this, and knowing how close to discovery we already were, I decided to confide in him and enlist his aid; so I told him. I hope you do not feel that I did wrong, Carson."

"By no means," I assured him. "We have been forced to tell others of our plans whom we knew and trusted less well than you know and trust your friend. What did he say when you had told him?"

"He said that he would help us, and that when we struck he would join us. He promised, too, that many others of the soldiers would do likewise; but the most important thing he did was to give me a key to the armory."

"Good!" I exclaimed. "There is no reason now why we should not strike at once."

"Tonight?" asked Zog eagerly.

"Tonight!" I replied. "Pass the word to Gamfor and Honan, and you four to the other Soldiers of Liberty."

We all laughed heartily, as though some one had told a most amusing story, and then Kiron and Zog left me, to acquaint Gamfor and Honan with our plan.

But upon Venus as upon earth, the best laid plans of mice and men "gang aft a-gley," which is slang for haywire. Every night since we had sailed from the harbor of Vepaja the hatch had been left off our ill-smelling prison to afford us ventilation, a single member of the watch patrolling near to see that none of us came out; but tonight the hatch was closed.

"This," growled Kiron, "is the result of Anoos's work."

"We shall have to strike by daylight," I whispered, "but we cannot pass the word tonight. It is so dark down here that we should certainly be overheard by some one outside our own number if we attempted it."

"Tomorrow then," said Kiron.

I was a long time getting to sleep that night, for my mind was troubled by fears for our entire plan. It was obvious now that the captain was suspicious, and that while he might not know anything of the details of what we purposed, he did know that something was in the air, and he was taking no chances.

During the night, as I lay awake trying to plan for the morrow, I heard some one prowling around the room, and now and again a whisper. I could only wonder who it was and try to guess what he was about. I recalled the bottle of wine that Anoos was supposed to have, and it occurred to me that he might be giving a party, but the voices were too subdued to bear out that theory. Finally I heard a muffled cry, a noise that sounded like a brief scuffle, and then silence again fell upon the chamber.

"Some one had a bad dream," I thought and fell asleep.

Morning came at last, and the hatch was removed, letting a little light in to dissipate the gloom of our prison. A sailor lowered a basket containing the food for our meager breakfast. We gathered about it and each took his share, and moved away to eat it, when suddenly there was a cry from the far side of the room.

"Look what's here!" the man shouted. "Anoos has been murdered!"

CHAPTER TEN

Mutiny

Yes, Anoos had been murdered, and there was a great hue and cry, much more of a hue and cry, it seemed to me, than the death of an ordinary prisoner should have aroused. Officers and soldiers swarmed in our quarters. They found Anoos stretched out on his back, a bottle of wine at his side. His throat was discolored where powerful fingers had crushed it. Anoos had been choked to death.

Soon they herded us on deck, where we were searched for weapons following an order from the captain of the ship, who had come forward to conduct an investigation. He was angry and excited and, I believe, somewhat frightened. One by one, he questioned us. When it was my turn to be questioned, I did not tell him what I had heard during the night; I told him that I had slept all night on the far side of the room from where Anoos's body was discovered.

"Were you acquainted with the dead man?" he asked.

"No more so than with any of the other prisoners," I replied.

"But you are very well acquainted with some of them," he said rather pointedly, I thought. "Have you ever spoken with the man?"

"Yes, he has talked to me on several occasions.

"About what?" demanded the captain.

"Principally about his grievances against the Thorists."

"But he was a Thorist," exclaimed the captain.

I knew that he was trying to pump me to discover if I harbored any suspicions concerning the actual status of Anoos, but he was not clever enough to succeed. "I certainly would never had suspected it from his conversation," I replied. "If he were a Thorist, he must have been a traitor to his country, for he continually sought to enlist my interest in a plan to seize the ship and murder all her officers. I think he approached others, also." I spoke in a tone loud enough to be heard by all, for I wanted the Soldiers of Liberty to take the cue from me. If enough of us told the same story it might convince the officers that Anoos's tale of a conspiracy was hatched in his own brain and worked up by his own efforts in an attempt to reap commendation and reward from his superiors, a trick by no means foreign to the ethics of spies.

"Did he succeed in persuading any of the prisoners to join him?" asked the captain.

"I think not; they all laughed at him."

"Have you any idea who murdered him?"

"Probably some patriot who resented his treason," I lied glibly.

As he questioned the other men along similar lines, I was pleased to discover that nearly every one of the Soldiers of Liberty had been approached by the perfidious Anoos, whose traitorous overtures they had virtuously repulsed. Zog said that he had never talked with the man, which, to the best of my knowledge, was the truth.

When the captain finished his investigation, he was farther from the truth than when he commenced it, for I am certain that he went aft convinced that there had been no truth in the tales that Anoos had carried to him.

I had been considerably worried at the time we were being searched, for fear that the key to the armory would be discovered on Kiron, but it had not been, and later he told me that he had hidden it in his hair the night before as a precaution against just such an eventuality as had occurred.

The Amtorian day consists of 26 hours, 56 minutes, 4 seconds of earth time, which the Amtorians divide into twenty equal periods called te, which, for clarity, I shall translate into its nearest earthly equivalent, hour, although it contains 80.895 earth minutes. On shipboard, the hours are sounded by a trumpeter, there being a distinguishing bar of music for each hour of the day. The first hour, or one o'clock, corresponds to mean sunrise. It is then that the prisoners are awakened and given food; forty minutes later they start work, which continues until the tenth hour, with a short recess for food in the middle of the day. Occasionally we were allowed to quit work at the ninth and even the eighth hour, according to the caprices of our masters.

On this day the Soldiers of Liberty congregated during the midday rest period, and, my mind being definitely determined on immediate action, I passed the word around that we would strike during the afternoon at the moment the trumpeter sounded the seventh hour. As many of us as were working aft near the armory were to make a dash for it with Kiron, who would unlock it in the event that it were locked. The remainder were to attack the soldiers nearest them with anything that they could use as weapons, or with their bare hands if they had no weapons, and take the soldiers' pistols and swords from them. Five of us were to account for the officers. Half of our number was to constantly shout our battle cry, "For liberty!" The other half was instructed to urge the remaining prisoners and the soldiers to join us.

It was a mad scheme and one in which only desperate men could have found hope.

The seventh hour was chosen because at that time the officers were nearly all congregated in the wardroom, where a light meal and wine were served them daily. We should have preferred launching our plan at night, but we feared a continuation of the practice of locking us below deck would prevent, and our experience with Anoos had taught us that we might expect the whole conspiracy to be divulged by another spy at any time; therefore we dared not wait.

I must confess to a feeling of increasing excitement as the hour approached. As, from time to time, I glanced at the other members of our little band, I thought that I could note signs of nervousness in some of them, while others worked on as placidly as though nothing unusual was about to occur. Zog was one of these. He was working near me. He never glanced toward the tower deck from which the trumpeter would presently sound the fateful notes, though it was with difficulty that I kept my eyes from it at all. No one would have thought that Zog was planning to attack the soldier lolling near him, nor have imagined that the night before he had murdered a man. He was humming a tune, as he polished the barrel of the big gun on which he was working.

Gamfor and, fortunately, Kiron were working aft, scrubbing the deck, and I saw that Kiron kept scrubbing closer and closer to the door of the armory. How I wished for Kamlot as the crucial moment approached! He could have done so much to insure the success of our *coup,* and yet he did not even know that such a stroke was contemplated, much less that it was so soon to be launched.

As I glanced about, I met Zog's gaze. Very solemnly he closed his left eye. At last he had given a sign that he was alert and ready. It was a little thing, but it put new heart into me. For some reason, during the past half hour I had felt very much alone.

The time was approaching the zero hour. I moved closer to my guard, so that I stood directly in front of him with my back toward him. I knew precisely what I was going to do, and I knew that it would be successful. Little did the man behind me dream that in a minute, or perhaps a few seconds, he would be lying senseless on the deck, or that the man he guarded would be carrying his sword, his dagger, and his pistol as the last notes of the seventh hour floated sweetly out across the calm waters of this Amtorian sea.

My back was now toward the deck houses. I could not see the trumpeter when he emerged from the tower to sound the hour, but I knew that it could not be long now before he stepped out onto the tower deck. Yet when the first note sounded I was as startled as though I had expected it never to sound. I presume it was the reaction after the long period of nervous tension.

My nervousness, however, was all mental; it did not affect my physical reactions to the needs of the moment. As the first note came softly down to my awaiting ears, I pivoted on a heel and swung my right for the chin of my unsuspecting guard. It was one of those blows that is often described as a haymaker, and it made hay. The fellow dropped in his tracks. As I stooped to recover his arms, pandemonium broke loose upon the deck. There were shrieks and groans and curses, and above all rose the war cry of the Soldiers of Liberty—my band had struck, and it had struck hard.

For the first time now, I heard the weird staccato hiss of Amtorian firearms. You have heard an X-ray machine in operation? It was like that, but louder and more sinister. I had wrenched the sword and pistol from the scabbard and holster of my fallen guard, not taking the time to remove his belt. Now I faced the scene for which I had so long waited. I saw the powerful Zog wrest the weapons from a soldier, and then lift the man's body above his head and cast it overboard. Evidently Zog had no time for proselyting.

At the door to the armory a battle was being waged; men were trying to enter, and soldiers were shooting them down. I ran in that direction. A soldier leaped in front of me, and I heard the hiss of the death rays that must have passed close to my body, as he tried to stop me. He must have been either nervous or a very poor shot, for he missed me. I turned my own weapon upon him and pressed the lever. The man slumped to the deck with a hole in his chest, and I ran on.

The fight at the door of the armory was hand to hand with swords, daggers, and fists, for by now the members of the two factions were so intermingled that none dared use a firearm for fear of injuring a comrade. Into this mêlée I leaped. Tucking the pistol into the band of my G string, I ran my sword through a great brute who was about to knife Honan; then I grabbed another by the hair and dragged him from the door, shouting to Honan to finish him—it took too long to run a sword into a man and then pull it out again. What I wanted was to get into the armory to Kiron's side and help him.

All the time I could hear my men shouting, "For liberty!" or urging the soldiers to join us—as far as I had been able to judge, all the prisoners had already done so. Now another soldier barred my way. His back was toward me, and I was about to seize him and hurl him back to Honan and the others who were fighting at his side, when I saw him slip his dagger into the heart of a soldier in front of him and, as he did so, cry, "For liberty!" Here was one convert at least. I did not know it then, but at that time there were already many such.

When I finally got into the armory, I found Kiron issuing arms as fast as he could pass them out. Many of the mutineers were crawling through the windows of the room to get weapons, and to each of these

Kiron passed several swords and pistols, directing the men to distribute them on deck.

Seeing that all was right here, I gathered a handful of men and started up the companionway to the upper decks, from which the officers were firing down upon the mutineers and, I may say, upon their own men as well. In fact, it was this heartless and stupid procedure that swung many of the soldiers to our side. Almost the first man I saw as I leaped to the level of the second deck was Kamlot. He had a sword in one hand and a pistol in the other, and he was firing rapidly at a group of officers who were evidently attempting to reach the main deck to take command of the loyal soldiers there.

You may be assured that it did my heart good to see my friend again, and as I ran to his side and opened fire on the officers, he flashed me a quick smile of recognition.

Three of the five officers opposing us had fallen, and now the remaining two turned and fled up the companionway to the top deck. Behind us were twenty or more mutineers eager to reach the highest deck, where all the surviving officers had now taken refuge, and I could see more mutineers crowding up the companionway from the main deck to join their fellows. Kamlot and I led the way to the next deck, but at the head of the companionway the surging mob of howling, cursing mutineers brushed past us to hurl themselves upon the officers.

The men were absolutely out of control, and as there were but few of my original little band of Soldiers of Liberty among them, the majority of them knew no leader, with the result that it was every man for himself. I wished to protect the officers, and it had been my intention to do so; but I was helpless to avert the bloody orgy that ensued with a resulting loss of life entirely disproportionate to the needs of the occasion.

The officers, fighting for their lives with their backs against a wall, took heavy toll of the mutineers, but they were eventually overwhelmed by superior numbers. Each of the common soldiers and sailors appeared to have a special grudge to settle either with some individual officer or with them all as a class and for the time all were transformed into maniacal furies, as time and again they charged the last fortress of authority, the oval tower on the upper deck.

Each officer that fell, either killed or wounded, was hurled over the rail to the deck below, where willing hands cast the body to the main deck from which, in turn, it was thrown into the sea. And then, at last, the mutineers gained access to the tower, from which they dragged the remaining officers, butchering them on the upper deck or hurling them to their shrieking fellows below.

The captain was the last to be dragged out. They had found him hiding in a cupboard in his cabin. At sight of him arose such a scream of hate and rage as I hope never to hear again. Kamlot and I were standing at one side, helpless witnesses of this holocaust of hate. We saw them literally tear the captain to pieces and cast him into the sea.

With the death of the captain the battle was over, the ship was ours. My plan had succeeded, but the thought suddenly assailed me that I had created a terrible power that it might be beyond me to control. I touched Kamlot on the arm. "Follow me," I directed and started for the main deck.

"Who is at the bottom of this?" asked Kamlot as we forced our way among the excited mutineers.

"The mutiny was my plan, but not the massacre," I replied. "Now we must attempt to restore order out of chaos."

"If we can," he remarked dubiously.

As I made my way toward the main deck, I collected as many of the original band of Soldiers of Liberty as we passed, and when I finally reached my destination, I gathered most of them about me. Among the mutineers I had discovered the trumpeter who had unknowingly sounded the signal for the outbreak, and him I caused to sound the call that should assemble all hands on the main deck. Whether or not the notes of the trumpet would be obeyed, I did not know, but so strong is the habit of discipline among trained men that immediately the call sounded the men began to pour onto the deck from all parts of the vessel.

I mounted the breech of one of the guns, and, surrounded by my faithful band, I announced that the Soldiers of Liberty had taken over the ship, that those who wished to accompany us must obey the vookor of the band; the others would be put ashore.

"Who is vookor?" demanded a soldier whom I recognized as one of those who had been most violent in the attack upon the officers.

"I am," I replied.

"The vookor should be one of us," he growled.

"Carson planned the mutiny and carried it to success," shouted Kiron. "Carson is vookor."

From the throats of all my original band and from a hundred new recruits rose a cheer of approval, but there were many who remained silent or spoke in grumbling undertones to those nearest them. Among these was Kodj, the soldier who had objected to my leadership, and I saw that already a faction was gathering about him.

"It is necessary," I said, "that all men return at once to their duties, for the ship must be handled, no matter who commands. If there is any question about leadership, that can be settled later. In the meantime, I am in command; Kamlot, Gamfor, Kiron, Zog, and Honan are my lieutenants; with me, they will officer the ship. All weapons must be turned over immediately to Kiron at the armory, except those carried by men regularly detailed by him for guard duty."

"No one is going to disarm me," blustered Kodj. "I have as much right to carry weapons as anyone. We are all free men now. I take orders from no one."

Zog, who had edged closer to him as he spoke, seized him by the throat with one of his huge hands and with the other tore the belt from about his hips. "You take orders from the new vookor or you go overboard," he growled, as he released the man and handed his weapons to Kiron.

For a moment there was silence, and there was a tenseness in the situation that boded ill; then some one laughed and cried, "No one is going to disarm me," mimicking Kodj. That brought a general laugh, and I knew that for the time being the danger was over. Kiron, sensing that the moment was ripe, ordered the men to come to the armory and turn in their weapons, and the remainder of the original band herded them aft in his wake.

It was an hour before even a semblance of order or routine had been reestablished. Kamlot, Gamfor, and I were gathered in the chart room in the tower. Our consort was hull down below the horizon, and we were discussing the means that should be adopted to capture her without bloodshed and rescue Duare and the other Vepajan prisoners aboard her. The idea had been in my mind from the very inception of the plan to seize our own ship, and it had been the first subject that Kamlot had broached after we had succeeded in quieting the men and restoring order; but Gamfor was frankly dubious concerning the feasibility of the project.

"The men are not interested in the welfare of Vepajans," he reminded us, "and they may resent the idea of endangering their lives and risking their new-found liberty in a venture that means nothing whatever to them."

"How do you feel about it, personally?" I asked him.

"I am under your orders," he replied; "I will do anything that you command, but I am only one—you have two hundred whose wishes you must consult."

"I shall consult only my officers," I replied; "to the others, I shall issue orders."

"That is the only way," said Kamlot in a tone of relief.

"Inform the other officers that we shall attack the *Sovong* at daybreak," I instructed them.

"But we dare not fire on her," protested Kamlot, "lest we endanger the life of Duare."

"I intend boarding her," I replied. "There will be no one but the watch on deck at that hour. On two other occasions the ships have been brought close together on a calm sea; so our approach will arouse no suspicion. The boarding party will consist of a hundred men who will remain concealed until the command to board is given when the ships are alongside one another. At that hour in the morning the sea is usually calm; if it is not calm tomorrow morning we shall have to postpone the attack until another morning.

"Issue strict orders that there is to be no slaughter; no one is to be killed who does not resist. We shall remove all of the *Sovong's* small arms and the bulk of her provisions, as well as the Vepajan prisoners, to the *Sofal*."

"And then what do you propose doing?" asked Gamfor.

"I am coming to that," I replied, "but first I wish to ascertain the temper of the men aboard the *Sofal*. You and Kamlot will inform the other officers of my plans insofar as I have explained them; then assemble the original members of the Soldiers of Liberty and explain my intentions to them. When this has been done, instruct them to disseminate the information among the remainder of the ship's company, reporting to you the names of all those who do not receive the plan with favor. These we shall leave aboard the *Sovong* with any others who may elect to transfer to her. At the eleventh hour muster the men on the main deck. At that time I will explain my plans in detail."

After Kamlot and Gamfor had departed to carry out my orders, I returned to the chart room. The *Sofal,* moving ahead at increased speed, was slowly overhauling the *Sovong,* though not at a rate that might suggest pursuit. I was certain that the *Sovong* knew nothing of what had transpired upon her sister ship, for the Amtorians are unacquainted with wireless communication, and there had been no time for the officers of the *Sofal* to signal their fellows aboard the *Sovong,* so suddenly had the mutiny broken and so quickly had it been carried to a conclusion.

As the eleventh hour approached, I noticed little groups of men congregated in different parts of the ship, evidently discussing the information that the Soldiers of Liberty had spread among them. One group, larger than the others, was being violently harangued by a loud-mouthed orator whom I recognized as Kodj. It had been apparent from the first that the fellow was a trouble maker. Just how much influence he had, I did not know; but I felt that whatever it was, it would be used against me. I hoped to be rid of him after we had taken the *Sovong.*

The men congregated rapidly as the trumpeter sounded the hour, and I came down the companionway to address them. I stood just above them, on one of the lower steps, where I could overlook them and be seen by all. Most of them were quiet and appeared attentive. There was one small group muttering and whispering—Kodj was its center.

"At daybreak we shall board and take the *Sovong,*" I commenced. "You will receive your orders from your immediate officers, but I wish to emphasize one in particular—there is to be no unnecessary killing. After we have taken the ship we shall transfer to the *Sofal* such provisions, weapons, and prisoners as we wish to take with us. At this time, also, we shall transfer from the *Sofal* to the *Sovong* all of you who do not wish to remain on this ship under my command, as well as those whom

I do not care to take with me," and as I said this, I looked straight at Kodj and the malcontents surrounding him.

"I shall explain what I have in mind for the future, so that each of you may be able to determine between now and daybreak whether he cares to become a member of my company. Those who do will be required to obey orders; but they will share in the profits of the cruise, if there are profits. The purposes of the expedition are twofold: To prey on Thorist shipping and to explore the unknown portions of Amtor after we have returned the Vepajan prisoners to their own country.

"There will be excitement and adventure; there will be danger, too; and I want no cowards along, nor any trouble makers. There should be profits, for I am assured that richly laden Thorist ships constantly ply the known seas of Amtor; and I am informed that we can always find a ready market for such spoils of war as fall into our hands—and war it shall be, with the Soldiers of Liberty fighting the oppression and tyranny of Thorism.

"Return to your quarters now, and be prepared to give a good account of yourselves at daybreak."

CHAPTER ELEVEN

Duare

I got little sleep that night. My officers were constantly coming to me with reports. From these I learned, what was of the greatest importance to me, the temper of the crew. None was averse to taking the *Sovong,* but there was a divergence of opinion as to what we should do thereafter. A few wanted to be landed on Thoran soil, so that they could make their way back to their homes; the majority was enthusiastic about plundering merchant ships; the idea of exploring the unknown waters of Amtor filled most of them with fear; some were averse to restoring the Vepajan prisoners to their own country; and there was an active and extremely vocal minority that insisted that the command of the vessel should be placed in the hands of Thorans. In this I could see the hand of Kodj even before they told me that the suggestion had come from the coterie that formed his following.

"But there are fully a hundred," said Gamfor, "upon whose loyalty you may depend: These have accepted you as their leader, and they will follow you and obey your commands."

"Arm these," I directed, "and place all others below deck until after we have taken the *Sovong.* How about the klangan? They took no part in the mutiny. Are they for us or against us?"

Kiron laughed. "They received no orders one way or the other," he explained. "They have no initiative. Unless they are motivated by such primitive instincts as hunger, love, or hate, they do nothing without orders from a superior."

"And they don't care who their master is," interjected Zog. "They serve loyally enough until their master dies, or sells them, or gives them away, or is overthrown; then they transfer the same loyalty to a new master."

"They have been told that you are their new master," said Kamlot, "and they will obey you."

As there were only five of the birdmen aboard the *Sofal,* I had not been greatly exercised about their stand; but I was glad to learn that they would not be antagonistic.

At the twentieth hour I ordered the hundred upon whom we could depend assembled and held in the lower deck house, the others having all been confined below earlier in the night, in the accomplishment of which a second mutiny was averted only by the fact that all the men had been previously disarmed except the loyal Soldiers of Liberty.

All during the night we had been gradually gaining upon the unsuspecting *Sovong* until now we were scarcely a hundred yards astern of her, slightly aport. Across our starbord bow I could see her looming darkly in the mysterious nocturnal glow of the moonless Amtorian night, her lanterns white and colored points of light, her watch dimly visible upon her decks.

Closer and closer the *Sofal* crept toward her prey. A Soldier of Liberty, who had once been an officer in the Thoran navy, was at the wheel; no one was on deck but the members of the watch; in the lower deck house a hundred men were huddled waiting for the command to board; I stood beside Honan in the chart room (he was to command the *Sofal* while I led the boarding party), my eyes upon the strange Amtorian chronometer. I spoke a word to him and he moved a lever. The *Sofal* crept a little closer to the *Sovong.* Then Honan whispered an order to the helmsman and we closed in upon our prey.

I hastened down the companionway to the main deck and gave the signal to Kamlot standing in the doorway of the deck house. The two ships were close now and almost abreast. The sea was calm; only a gentle swell raised and lowered the softly gliding ships. Now we were so close that a man could step across the intervening space from the deck of one ship to that of the other.

The officer of the watch aboard the *Sovong* hailed us. "What are you about?" he demanded. "Sheer off, there!"

For answer I ran across the deck of the *Sofal* and leaped aboard the other ship, a hundred silent men following in my wake. There was no shouting and little noise—only the shuffling of sandalled feet and the subdued clank of arms.

Behind us the grappling hooks were thrown over the rail of the *Sovong*. Every man had been instructed as to the part he was to play. Leaving Kamlot in command on the main deck, I ran to the tower deck with a dozen men, while Kiron led a score of fighting men to the second deck where most of the officers were quartered.

Before the officer of the watch could gather his scattered wits, I had him covered with a pistol. "Keep quiet," I whispered, "and you will not be harmed." My plan was to take as many of them as possible before a general alarm could be sounded and thus minimize the necessity for bloodshed; therefore, the need for silence. I turned him over to one of my men after disarming him; and then I sought the captain, while two of my detachment attended to the helmsman.

I found the officer for whom I sought reaching for his weapons. He had been awakened by the unavoidable noise of the boarding party, and, suspecting that something was amiss, had seized his weapons as he arose and uncovered the lights in his cabin.

I was upon him as he raised his pistol, and struck it from his hand before he could fire; but he stepped back with his sword on guard, and thus we stood facing one another for a moment.

"Surrender," I told him, "and you will not be harmed."

"Who are you?" he demanded, "and where did you come from?"

"I was a prisoner on board the *Sofal*," I replied, "but now I command her. If you wish to avoid bloodshed, come out on deck with me and give the command to surrender."

"And then what?" he demanded. "Why have you boarded us if not to kill?"

"To take off provisions, weapons, and the Vepajan prisoners," I explained.

Suddenly the hissing staccato of pistol fire came up to us from the deck below.

"I thought there was to be no killing!" he snapped.

"If you want to stop it, get out there and give the command to surrender," I replied.

"I don't believe you," he cried. "It's a trick," and he came at me with his sword.

I did not wish to shoot him down in cold blood, and so I met his attack with my own blade. The advantage was on his side in the matter of skill, for I had not yet fully accustomed myself to the use of the Amtorian sword; but I had an advantage in strength and reach and in some tricks of German swordplay that I had learned while I was in Germany.

The Amtorian sword is primarily a cutting weapon, its weight near the tip making it particularly effective for this method of attack, though it lessens its effectiveness in parrying thrusts, rendering it a rather sluggish defensive weapon. I therefore found myself facing a savage cutting attack against which I had difficulty in defending myself. The officer was an active man and skillful with the sword. Being experienced, it did not take him long to discover that I was a novice, with the result that he pressed his advantage viciously, so that I soon regretted my magnanimity in not resorting to my pistol before the encounter began; but it was too late now—the fellow kept me so busy that I had no opportunity to draw the weapon.

He forced me back and around the room until he stood between me and the doorway, and then, having me where no chance for escape remained, he set to work to finish me with dispatch. The duel, as far as I was concerned, was fought wholly on the defensive. So swift and persistent was his attack that I could only defend myself, and not once in the first two minutes of the encounter did I aim a single blow at him.

I wondered what had become of the men who had accompanied me; but pride would not permit me to call upon them for help, nor did I learn until later that it would have availed me nothing, since they were having all that they could attend to in repelling the attack of several officers who had run up from below immediately behind them.

The teeth of my antagonist were bared in a grim and ferocious smile, as he battered relentlessly at my guard, as though he already sensed victory and was gloating in anticipation. The clanging of steel on steel now drowned all sounds from beyond the four walls of the cabin where we fought; I could not tell if fighting were continuing in other parts of the ship, nor, if it were, whether it were going in our favor or against us. I realized that I *must* know these things, that I was responsible for whatever took place aboard the *Sovong,* and that I must get out of that cabin and lead my men either in victory or defeat.

Such thoughts made my position even more impossible than as though only my life were at stake and drove me to attempt heroic measures for releasing myself from my predicament and my peril. I must destroy my adversary, and I must do so at once!

He had me now with my back almost against the wall. Already his point had touched me upon the cheek once and twice upon the body, and though the wounds were but scratches, I was covered with blood. Now he leaped upon me in a frenzy of determination to have done with me instantly, but this time I did not fall back. I parried his cut, so that his sword passed to the right of my body which was now close to his; and then I drew back my point, and, before he could recover himself, drove it through his heart.

As he sagged to the floor, I jerked my sword from his body and ran from his cabin. The entire episode had required but a few minutes, though it had seemed much longer to me, yet in that brief time much had occurred on the decks and in the cabins of the *Sovong.* The upper decks were cleared of living enemies; one of my own men was at the wheel, another at the controls; there was still fighting on the main deck where some of the *Sovong's* officers were making a desperate last stand with a handful of their men. But by the time I reached the scene of the battle, it was over; the officers, assured by Kamlot that their lives would be spared, had surrendered—the *Sovong* was ours. The *Sofal* had taken her first prize!

As I sprang into the midst of the excited warriors on the main deck, I must have presented a sorry spectacle, bleeding, as I was, from my three wounds; but my men greeted me with loud cheers. I learned later that my absence from the fighting on the main deck had been noticed

and had made a poor impression on my men, but when they saw me return bearing the scars of combat, my place in their esteem was secured. Those three little scratches proved of great value to me, but they were as nothing in comparison with the psychological effect produced by the wholly disproportionate amount of blood they had spilled upon my naked hide.

We now quickly rounded up our prisoners and disarmed them. Kamlot took a detachment of men and released the Vepajan captives whom he transferred at once to the *Sofal.* They were nearly all women, but I did not see them as they were taken from the ship, being engaged with other matters. I could imagine, though, the joy in the hearts of Kamlot and Duare at this reunion, which the latter at least had probably never even dared to hope for.

Rapidly we transferred all of the small arms of the *Sovong* to the *Sofal,* leaving only sufficient to equip the officers of the ill-starred vessel. This work was intrusted to Kiron and was carried out by our own men, while Gamfor, with a contingent of our new-made prisoners, carried all of the *Sovong's* surplus provisions aboard our own ship. This done, I ordered all the *Sovong's* guns thrown overboard—by that much at least I would cripple the power of Thora. The last act in this drama of the sea was to march our one hundred imprisoned malcontents from the *Sofal* to the *Sovong* and present them to the latter's new commander with my compliments. He did not seem greatly pleased, however, nor could I blame him. Neither were the prisoners pleased. Many of them begged me to take them back aboard the *Sofal;* but I already had more men than I felt were needed to navigate and defend the ship; and each of the prisoners had been reported as having expressed disapproval of some part or all of our plan; so that I, who must have absolute loyalty and cooperation, considered them valueless to me.

Kodj, strange to say, was the most persistent. He almost went on his knees as he pleaded with me to permit him to remain with the *Sofal,* and he promised me such loyalty as man had never known before; but I had had enough of Kodj and told him so. Then, when he found that I could not be moved, he turned upon me, swearing by all his ancestors that he would get even with me yet, even though it took a thousand years.

Returning to the deck of the *Sofal,* I ordered the grappling hooks cast off; and presently the two ships were under way again, the *Sovong* proceeding toward the Thoran port that was her destination, the *Sofal* back toward Vepaja. Now, for the first time, I had opportunity to inquire into our losses and found that we had suffered four killed and twenty-one wounded, the casualties among the crew of the *Sovong* having been much higher.

For the greater part of the remainder of the day I was busy with my officers organizing the personnel of the *Sofal* and systematizing the activities of this new and unfamiliar venture, in which work Kiron and Gamfor were of inestimable value; and it was not until late in the afternoon that I had an opportunity to inquire into the welfare of the rescued Vepajan captives. When I asked Kamlot about them, he said that they were none the worse for their captivity aboard the *Sovong.*

"You see, these raiding parties have orders to bring the women to Thora unharmed and in good condition," he explained. "They are destined for more important persons than ships' officers, and that is their safeguard.

"However, Duare said that notwithstanding this, the captain made advances to her. I wish I might have known it while I was still aboard the *Sovong,* that I might have killed him for his presumption." Kamlot's tone was bitter and he showed signs of unusual excitement.

"Let your mind rest at ease," I begged him; "Duare has been avenged."

"What do you mean?"

"I killed the captain myself," I explained.

He clapped a hand upon my shoulder, his eyes alight with pleasure. "Again you have won the undying gratitude of Vepaja," he cried. "I wish that it might have been my good fortune to have killed the beast and thus wiped out the insult upon Vepaja, but if I could not be the one, then I am glad that it was you, Carson, rather than another."

I thought that he took the matter rather seriously and was placing too much importance upon the action of the *Sovong's* captain, since it had resulted in no harm to the girl; but then, of course, I realized that love plays strange tricks upon a man's mental processes, so that an affront to a mistress might be magnified to the proportions of a national calamity.

"Well, it is all over now," I said, "and your sweetheart has been returned to you safe and sound."

At that he looked horrified. "My sweetheart!" he exclaimed. "In the name of the ancestors of all the jongs! Do you mean to tell me that you do not know who Duare is?"

"I thought of course that she was the girl you loved," I confessed. "Who is she?"

"Of course I love her," he explained; "all Vepaja loves her—she is the virgin daughter of a Vepajan jong!"

Had he been announcing the presence of a goddess on shipboard, his tone could have been no more reverential and awed. I endeavored to appear more impressed than I was, lest I offend him.

"Had she been the woman of your choice," I said, "I should have been even more pleased to have had a part in her rescue than had she been the daughter of a dozen jongs."

"That is nice of you," he replied, "but do not let other Vepajans hear you say such things. You have told me of the divinities of that strange world from which you come; the persons of the jong and his children are similarly sacred to us."

"Then, of course, they shall be sacred to me," I assured him.

"By the way, I have word for you that should please you—a Vepajan would consider it a high honor. Duare desires to see you, that she may thank you personally. It is irregular, of course; but then circumstances have rendered strict adherence to the etiquette and customs of our country impracticable, if not impossible. Several hundred men already have looked upon her, many have spoken to her, and nearly all of them were enemies; so it can do no harm if she sees and speaks with her defenders and her friends."

I did not understand what he was driving at, but I assented to what he had said and told him that I would pay my respects to the princess before the day was over.

I was very busy; and, if the truth must be told, I was not particularly excited about visiting the princess. In fact, I rather dreaded it, for I am not particularly keen about fawning and kotowing to royalty or anything else; but I decided that out of respect for Kamlot's feelings I must get the thing over as soon as possible, and after he had left to attend to some duty, I made my way to the quarters allotted to Duare on the second deck.

The Amtorians do not knock on a door—they whistle. It is rather an improvement, I think, upon our custom. One has one's own distinctive whistle. Some of them are quite elaborate airs. One soons learns to recognize the signals of one's friends. A knock merely informs you that some one wishes to enter; a whistle tells you the same thing and also reveals the identity of your caller.

My signal, which is very simple, consists of two short low notes followed by a higher longer note; and as I stood before the door of Duare and sounded this, my mind was not upon the princess within but upon another girl far away in the tree city of Kooaad, in Vepaja. She was often in my mind—the girl whom I had glimpsed but twice, to whom I had spoken but once and that time to avow a love that had enveloped me as completely, spontaneously, and irrevocably as would death upon some future day.

In response to my signal a soft, feminine voice bade me enter. I stepped into the room and faced Duare. At sight of me her eyes went wide and a quick flush mounted her cheeks. "You!" she exclaimed.

I was equally dumfounded—she was the girl from the garden of the jong!

CHAPTER TWELVE

"A Ship!"

What a strange *contretemps!* Its suddenness left me temporarily speechless; the embarrassment of Duare was only too obvious. Yet it was that unusual paradox, a happy *contretemps*—for me at least.

I advanced toward her, and there must have been a great deal more in my eyes than I realized, for she shrank back, flushing even more deeply than before.

"Don't touch me!" she whispered. "Don't dare!"

"Have I ever harmed you?" I asked.

That question seemed to bring her confidence. She shook her head. "No," she admitted, "you never have—physically. I sent for you to thank you for the service you have already rendered me; but I did not know it was *you.* I did not know that the Carson they spoke of was the man who—" She stopped there and looked at me appealingly.

"The man who told you in the garden of the jong that he loved you," I prompted her.

"Don't!" she cried. "Can it be that you do not realize the offensiveness, the criminality of such a declaration?"

"Is it a crime to love you?" I asked.

"It is a crime to tell me so," she replied with something of haughtiness.

"Then I am a confirmed criminal," I replied, "for I cannot help telling you that I love you, whenever I see you."

"If that is the case, you must not see me again, for you must never again speak those words to me," she said decisively. "Because of the service you have rendered me, I forgive you your past offenses; but do not repeat them."

"What if I can't help it?" I inquired.

"You must help it," she stated seriously; "it is a matter of life and death to you."

Her words puzzled me. "I do not understand what you mean," I admitted.

"Kamlot, Honan, any of the Vepajans aboard this ship would kill you if they knew," she replied. "The jong, my father, would have you destroyed upon our return to Vepaja—it would all depend upon whom I told first."

I came a little closer to her and looked straight into her eyes. "You would never tell," I whispered.

"Why not? What makes you think that?" she demanded, but her voice quavered a little.

"Because you want me to love you," I challenged her.

She stamped her foot angrily. "You are beyond reason or forbearance or decency!" she exclaimed. "Leave my cabin at once; I do not wish ever to see you again."

Her bosom was heaving, her beautiful eyes were flashing, she was very close to me, and an impulse seized me to take her in my arms. I wanted to crush her body to mine, I wanted to cover her lips with kisses; but more than all else I wanted her love, and so I restrained myself, for fear that I might go too far and lose the chance to win the love that I felt was hovering just below the threshold of her consciousness. I do not know why I was so sure of that, but I was. I could not have brought myself to force my attentions upon a woman to whom they were repugnant, but from the first moment that I had seen this girl watching me from the garden in Vepaja, I had been impressed by an inner consciousness of her interest in me, her more than simple interest. It was just one of those things that are the children of old Chand Kabi's training, a training that has made me infinitely more intuitive than a woman.

"I am sorry that you are sending me away into virtual exile," I said. "I do not feel that I deserve that, but of course the standards of your world are not the standards of mine. There, a woman is not dishonored by the love of a man, or by its avowal, unless she is already married to another," and then of a sudden a thought occurred to me that should have occurred before. "Do you already belong to some man?" I demanded, chilled by the thought.

"Of course not!" she snapped. "I am not yet nineteen." I wondered that it had never before occurred to me that the girl in the garden of the jong might be already married.

I did not know what that had to do with it, but I was glad to learn that she was not seven hundred years old. I had often wondered about her age, though after all it could have made no difference, since on Venus, if anywhere in the universe, people are really no older than they look—I mean, as far as their attractiveness is concerned.

"Are you going?" she demanded, "or shall I have to call one of the Vepajans and tell them that you have affronted me?"

"And have me killed?" I asked. "No, you cannot make me believe that you would ever do that."

"Then *I* shall leave," she stated, "and remember that you are never to see me or speak to me again."

With that parting and far from cheering ultimatum she quit the room, going into another of her suite. That appeared to end the interview; I could not very well follow her, and so I turned and made my way disconsolately to the captain's cabin in the tower.

As I thought the matter over, it became obvious to me that I not only had not made much progress in my suit, but that there was little likelihood that I ever should. There seemed to be some insuperable barrier between us, though what it was I could not imagine. I could not believe that she was entirely indifferent to me; but perhaps that was just a reflection of my egotism, for I had to admit that she had certainly made it plain enough both by words and acts that she wished to have nothing to do with me. I was unquestionably *persona non grata.*

Notwithstanding all this, or maybe because of it, I realized that this second and longer interview had but served to raise my passion to still greater heat, leaving me in a fine state of despair. Her near presence on board the *Sofal* was constantly provocative, while her interdiction of any relations between us only tended to make me more anxious to be with her. I was most unhappy, and the monotony of the now uneventful voyage back toward Vepaja offered no means of distraction. I wished that we might sight another vessel, for any ship that we sighted would be an enemy ship. We were outlaws, we of the *Sofal*—pirates, buccaneers, privateers. I rather leaned toward the last and most polite definition of our status. Of course we had not as yet been commissioned by Mintep to raid shipping for Vepaja, but we were striking at Vepaja's enemies, and so I felt that we had some claim upon the dubious respectability of privateerism. However, either of the other two titles would not have greatly depressed me. Buccaneer has a devil-may-care ring to it that appeals to my fancy; it has a trifle more *haut ton* than pirate.

There is much in a name. I had liked the name of the *Sofal* from the first. Perhaps it was the psychology of that name that suggested the career upon which I was now launched. It means killer. The verb meaning kill is *fal.* The prefix *so* has the same value as the suffix *er* in English; so sofal means killer. *Vong* is the Amtorian word for defend; therefore, *Sovong,* the name of our first prize, means defender; but the *Sovong* had not lived up to her name.

I was still meditating on names in an effort to forget Duare, when Kamlot joined me, and I decided to take the opportunity to ask him some questions concerning certain Amtorian customs that regulated the social intercourse between men and maids. He opened a way to the subject by asking me if I had seen Duare since she sent for me.

"I saw her," I replied, "but I do not understand her attitude, which suggested that it was almost a crime for me to look at her."

"It would be under ordinary circumstances," he told me, "but of course, as I explained to you before, what she and we have passed through has temporarily at least minimized the importance of certain time-honored Vepajan laws and customs.

"Vepajan girls attain their majority at the age of twenty; prior to that they may not form a union with a man. The custom, which has almost the force of a law, places even greater restrictions upon the daughters of a jong. They may not even see or speak to any man other than their blood relatives and a few well-chosen retainers until after they have reached their twentieth birthday. Should they transgress, it would mean disgrace for them and death for the man."

"What a fool law!" I ejacuated, but I realized at last how heinous my transgression must have appeared in the eyes of Duare.

Kamlot shrugged. "It may be a fool law," he said, "but it is still the law; and in the case of Duare its enforcement means much to Vepaja, for she is the hope of Vepaja."

I had heard that title conferred upon her before, but it was meaningless to me. "Just what do you mean by saying that she is the hope of Vepaja?" I asked.

"She is Mintep's only child. He has never had a son, though a hundred women have sought to bear him one. The life of the dynasty ends if Duare bears no son; and if she is to bear a son, then it is essential that the father of that son be one fitted to be the father of a jong."

"Have they selected the father of her children yet?" I asked.

"Of course not," replied Kamlot. "The matter will not even be broached until after Duare has passed her twentieth birthday."

"And she is not even nineteen yet," I remarked with a sigh.

"No," agreed Kamlot, eyeing me closely, "but you act as though that fact were of importance to you."

"It is," I admitted.

"What do you mean?" he demanded.

"I intend to marry Duare!"

Kamlot leaped to his feet and whipped out his sword. It was the first time that I had ever seen him show marked excitement. I thought he was going to kill me on the spot.

"Defend yourself!" he cried. "I cannot kill you until you draw."

"Just why do you wish to kill me at all?" I demanded. "Have you gone crazy?"

The point of Kamlot's sword dropped slowly toward the floor. "I do not wish to kill you," he said rather sadly, all the nervous excitement gone from his manner. "You are my friend, you have saved my life—no, I would rather die myself than kill you, but the thing you have just said demands it."

I shrugged my shoulders; the thing was inexplicable to me. "What did I say that demands death?" I demanded.

"That you intend to marry Duare."

"In my world," I told him, "men are killed for saying that they do *not* intend marrying some girl." I had been sitting at the desk in my cabin at the time that Kamlot had threatened me, and I had not arisen; now I stood up and faced him. "You had better kill me, Kamlot," I said, "for I spoke the truth."

He hesitated for a moment, standing there looking at me; then he returned his sword to its scabbard. "I cannot," he said huskily. "May my ancestors forgive me! I cannot kill my friend.

"Perhaps," he added, seeking some extenuating circumstance, "you should not be held accountable to customs of which you had no knowledge. I often forget that you are of another world than ours. But tell me, now that I have made myself a party to your crime by excusing it, what leads you to believe that you will marry Duare? I can incriminate myself no more by listening to you further."

"I intend to marry her, because I know that I love her and believe that she already half loves me."

At this Kamlot appeared shocked and horrified again. "That is impossible," he cried. "She never saw you before; she cannot dream what is in your heart or your mad brain."

"On the contrary, she has seen me before; and she knows quite well what is in my 'mad brain,'" I assured him. "I told her in Kooaad; I told her again today."

"And she listened?"

"She was shocked," I admitted, "but she listened; then she upbraided me and ordered me from her presence."

Kamlot breathed a sigh of relief. "At least *she* has not gone mad. I cannot understand on what you base your belief that she may return your love."

"Her eyes betrayed her; and, what may be more convincing, she did not expose my perfidy and thus send me to my death."

He pondered that and shook his head. "It is all madness," he said; "I can make nothing of it. You say that you talked with her in Kooaad, but that would have been impossible. But if you had ever even seen her before, why did you show so little interest in her fate when you knew that she was a prisoner aboard the *Sovong?* Why did you say that you thought that she was my sweetheart?"

"I did not know until a few minutes ago," I explained, "that the girl I saw and talked with in the garden at Kooaad was Duare, the daughter of the jong."

A few days later I was again talking with Kamlot in my cabin when we were interrupted by a whistle at the door; and when I had bade him do so, one of the Vepajan prisoners that we had rescued from the *Sovong* entered. He was not from Kooaad but from another city of Vepaja, and therefore none of the other Vepajans aboard knew anything concerning him. His name was Vilor, and he appeared to be a decent sort of fellow, though rather inclined to taciturnity. He had manifested considerable interest in the klangans and was with them often, but had explained this idiosyncrasy on the grounds that he was a scholar and wished to study the birdmen, specimens of which he had never before seen.

"I have come," he explained in response to my inquiry, "to ask you to appoint me an officer. I should like to join your company and share in the work and responsibilities of the expedition."

"We are well officered now," I explained, "and have all the men we need. Furthermore," I added frankly, "I do not know you well enough to be sure of your qualifications. By the time we reach Vejapa, we shall be better acquainted; and if I need you then, I will tell you."

"Well, I should like to do something," he insisted. "May I guard the janjong until we reach Vepaja?"

He referred to Duare, whose title, compounded of the two words daughter and king, is synonymous to princess. I thought that I noticed just a trace of excitement in his voice as he made the request.

"She is well guarded now," I explained. "But I should like to do it," he insisted. "It would be a service of love and loyalty for my jong. I could stand the night guard; no one likes that detail ordinarily."

"It will not be necessary," I said shortly; "the guard is already sufficient."

"She is in the after cabins of the second deck house, is she not?" he asked.

I told him that she was.

"And she has a special guard?"

"A man is always before her door at night," I assured him.

"Only one?" he demanded, as though he thought the guard insufficient.

"In addition to the regular watch, we consider one man enough; she has no enemies aboard the *Sofal*." These people were certainly solicitous of the welfare and safety of their royalty, I thought; and, it seemed to me, unnecessarily so. But finally Vilor gave up and departed, after begging me to give his request further thought.

"He seems even more concerned about the welfare of Duare than you," I remarked to Kamlot after Vilor had gone.

"Yes, I noticed that," replied my lieutenant thoughtfully.

"There is no one more concerned about her than I," I said, "but I cannot see that any further precautions are necessary."

"Nor I," agreed Kamlot; "she is quite well protected now."

We had dropped Vilor from our minds and were discussing other matters, when we heard the voice of the lookout in the crow's nest shouting, "Voo notar!" ("A ship!") Running to the tower deck, we got the bearings of the stranger as the lookout announced them the second time, and, sure enough, almost directly abeam on the starboard side we discerned the superstructure of a ship on the horizon.

For some reason which I do not clearly understand, the visibility on Venus is usually exceptionally good. Low fogs and haze are rare, notwithstanding the humidity of the atmosphere. This condition may be due to the mysterious radiation from that strange element in the planet's structure which illuminates her moonless nights; I do not know.

At any rate, we could see a ship, and almost immediately all was excitement aboard the *Sofal*. Here was another prize, and the men were eager to be at her. As we changed our course and headed for our victim, a cheer rose from the men on deck. Weapons were issued, the bow gun and the two tower guns were elevated to firing positions. The *Sofal* forged ahead at full speed.

As we approached our quarry, we saw that it was a ship of about the same size as the *Sofal* and bearing the insignia of Thora. Closer inspection revealed it to be an armed merchantman.

I now ordered all but the gunners into the lower deck house, as I planned on boarding this vessel as I had the *Sovong* and did not wish her to see our deck filled with armed men before we came alongside. As before, explicit orders were issued; every man knew what was expected of him; all were cautioned against needless killing. If I were to be a pirate, I was going to be as humane a pirate as possible. I would not spill blood needlessly.

I had questioned Kiron, Gamfor, and many another Thoran in my company relative to the customs and practices of Thoran ships of war until I felt reasonably familiar with them. I knew for instance that a warship might search a merchantman. It was upon this that I based my hope of getting our grappling hooks over the side of our victim before he could suspect our true design.

When we were within hailing distance of the ship, I directed Kiron to order her to shut down her engines, as we wished to board and search her; and right then we ran into our first obstacle. It came in the form of a pennant suddenly hoisted at the bow of our intended victim. It meant nothing to me, but it did to Kiron and the other Thorans aboard the *Sofal*.

"We'll not board her so easily after all," said Kiron. "She has an ongyan on board, and that exempts her from search. It probably also indicates that she carries a larger complement of soldiers than a merchantman ordinarily does."

"Whose friend?" I asked, "Yours?" for ongyan means great friend, in the sense of eminent or exalted.

Kiron smiled. "It is a title. There are a hundred klongyan in the oligarchy; one of them is aboard that ship. They are great friends unquestionably, great friends of themselves; they rule Thora more tyranically than any jong and for themselves alone."

"How will the men feel about attacking a ship bearing so exalted a personage?" I inquired.

"They will fight among themselves to be the first aboard and to run a sword through him."

"They must not kill him," I replied. "I have a better plan."

"They will be hard to control once they are in the thick of a fight," Kiron assured me; "I have yet to see the officer who can do it. In the old days, in the days of the jongs, there were order and discipline; but not now."

"There will be aboard the *Sofal,*" I averred. "Come with me; I am going to speak to the men."

Together we entered the lower deck house where the majority of the ship's company was massed, waiting for the command to attack. There were nearly a hundred rough and burly fighting men, nearly all of whom were ignorant and brutal. We had been together as commander and crew for too short a time for me to gauge their sentiments toward me; but I realized that there must be no question in any mind as to who was captain of the ship, no matter what they thought of me.

Kiron had called them to attention as we entered, and now every eye was on me as I started to speak. "We are about to take another ship," I began, "on board which is one whom Kiron tells me you will want to kill. He is an ongyan. I have come here to tell you that he must not be killed." Growls of disapproval greeted this statement, but, ignoring them, I continued, "I have come here to tell you something else, because I have been informed that no officer can control you after you enter battle. There are reasons why it will be better for us to hold this man prisoner than to kill him, but these have nothing to do with the question; what you must understand is that my orders and the orders of your other officers must be obeyed.

"We are embarked upon an enterprise that can succeed only if discipline be enforced. I expect the enterprise to succeed. I will enforce discipline. Insubordination or disobedience will be punishable by death. That is all."

As I left the room, I left behind me nearly a hundred silent men. There was nothing to indicate what their reaction had been. Purposely, I took Kiron out with me; I wanted the men to have an opportunity to discuss the matter among themselves without interference by an officer. I knew that I had no real authority over them, and that eventually they must decide for themselves whether they would obey me; the sooner that decision was reached the better for all of us.

Amtorian ships employ only the most primitive means of intercommunication. There is a crude and cumbersome hand signalling system in which flags are employed; then there is a standardized system of trumpet calls which covers a fairly wide range of conventional messages, but the most satisfactory medium and the one most used is the human voice.

Since our quarry had displayed the pennant of the ongyan, we had held a course parallel to hers and a little distance astern. On her main deck a company of armed men was congregated. She mounted four guns, which had been elevated into firing position. She was ready, but I think that as yet she suspected nothing wrong in our intentions.

Now I gave orders that caused the *Sofal* to close in upon the other ship, and as the distance between them lessened I saw indications of increasing excitement on the decks of our intended victim.

"What are you about?" shouted an officer from her tower deck. "Stand off there! There is an ongyan aboard us."

As no reply was made him, and as the *Sofal* continued to draw nearer, his excitement waxed. He gesticulated rapidly as he conversed with a fat man standing at his side; then he screamed, "Stand off or some one will suffer for this"; but the *Sofal* only moved steadily closer. "Stand off, or I'll fire!" shouted the captain.

For answer I caused all our starboard guns to be elevated into firing position. I knew he would not dare fire now, for a single broadside from the *Sofal* would have sunk him in less than a minute, a contingency which I wished to avoid as much as he.

"What do you want of us?" he demanded.

"We want to board you," I replied, "without bloodshed if possible."

"This is revolution! This is treason!" shouted the fat man at the captain's side. "I order you to stand off and leave us alone. I am the ongyan, Moosko," and then to the soldiers on the main deck he screamed, "Repel them! Kill any man who sets foot upon that deck!"

CHAPTER THIRTEEN

Catastrophe

At the same moment that the ongyan, Moosko, ordered his soldiers to repel any attempt to board his ship, her captain ordered full speed ahead and threw her helm to starboard. She veered away from us and leaped ahead in an effort to escape. Of course I could have sunk her, but her loot would have been of no value to me at the bottom of the sea; instead I directed the trumpeter at my side to sound full speed ahead to the officer in the tower, and the chase was on.

The *Yan,* whose name was now discernible across her stern, was much faster than Kiron had led me to believe; but the *Sofal* was exceptionally speedy, and it soon became obvious to all that the other ship could not escape her. Slowly we regained the distance that we had lost in the first, unexpected spurt of the *Yan*; slowly but surely we were closing up on her. Then the captain of the *Yan* did just what I should have done had I been in his place; he kept the *Sofal* always directly astern of him and opened fire on us with his after tower gun and with a gun similarly placed in the stern on the lower deck. The maneuver was tactically faultless, since it greatly reduced the number of guns that we could bring into play without changing our course, and was the only one that might offer him any hope of escape.

There was something eery in the sound of that first heavy Amtorian gun that I had heard. I saw nothing, neither smoke nor flame;

there was only a loud staccato roar more reminiscent of machine gun fire than of any other sound. At first there was no other effect; then I saw a piece of our starboard rail go and two of my men fall to the deck.

By this time our bow gun was in action. We were in the swell of the *Yan's* wake, which made accurate firing difficult. The two ships were racing ahead at full speed; the prow of the *Sofal* was throwing white water and spume far to either side; the sea in the wake of the *Yan* was boiling, and a heavy swell that we were quartering kept the ships rolling. The thrill of the chase and of battle was in our blood, and above all was the venomous rattle of the big guns.

I ran to the bow to direct the fire of the gun there, and a moment later we had the satisfaction of seeing the crew of one of the *Yan's* guns crumple to the deck man by man, as our gunner got his sights on them and mowed them down.

The *Sofal* was gaining rapidly upon the *Yan,* and our guns were concentrating on the tower gun and the tower of the enemy. The ongyan had long since disappeared from the upper deck, having doubtlessly sought safety in a less exposed part of the ship, and in fact there were only two men left alive upon the tower deck where he had stood beside the captain; these were two of the crew of the gun that was giving us most trouble.

I did not understand at the time why the guns of neither ship were more effective. I knew that the T-ray was supposedly highly destructive, and so I could not understand why neither ship had been demolished or sunk; but that was because I had not yet learned that all the vital parts of the ships were protected by a thin armor of the same metal of which the large guns were composed, the only substance at all impervious to the T-ray. Had this not been true, our fire would have long since put the *Yan* out of commission, as our T-rays, directed upon her after tower gun, would have passed on through the tower, killing the men at the controls and destroying the controls themselves. Eventually this would have happened, but it would have been necessary first to have destroyed the protective armor of the tower.

At last we succeeded in silencing the remaining gun, but if we were to draw up alongside the *Yan* we must expose ourselves to the fire of other guns located on her main deck and the forward end of the tower. We had already suffered some losses, and I knew that we must certainly expect a great many more if we put ourselves in range of those other guns; but there seemed no other alternative than to abandon the chase entirely, and that I had no mind to do.

Giving orders to draw up along her port side, I directed the fire of the bow gun along her rail where it would rake her port guns one by one as we moved up on her, and gave orders that each of our starboard guns in succession should open fire similarly as they came within range of the *Yan's* guns. Thus we kept a steady and continuous fire streaming upon the unhappy craft as we drew alongside her and closed up the distance between us.

We had suffered a number of casualties, but our losses were nothing compared to those of the *Yan,* whose decks were now strewn with dead and dying men. Her plight was hopeless, and her commander must at last have realized it, for now he gave the signal of surrender and stopped his engines. A few minutes later we were alongside and our boarding party had clambered over her rail.

As Kamlot and I stood watching these men who were being led by Kiron to take possession of the prize and bring certain prisoners aboard the *Sofal,* I could not but speculate upon what their answer was to be to my challenge for leadership. I knew that their freedom from the constant menace of their tyrannical masters was so new to them that they might well be expected to commit excesses, and I dreaded the result, for I had determined to make an example of any men who disobeyed me, though I fell in the attempt. I saw the majority of them spread over the deck under the command of the great Zog, while Kiron led a smaller detachment to the upper decks in search of the captain and the ongyan.

Fully five minutes must have elapsed before I saw my lieutenant emerge from the tower of the *Yan* with his two prisoners. He conducted them down the companionway and across the main deck toward the *Sofal,* while a hundred members of my pirate band watched them in silence. Not a hand was raised against them as they passed.

Kamlot breathed a sigh of relief as the two men clambered over the rail of the *Sofal* and approached us. "I think that our lives hung in the balance then, quite as much as theirs," he said, and I agreed with him, for if my men had started killing aboard the *Yan* in defiance of my orders, they would have had to kill me and those loyal to me to protect their own lives.

The ongyan was still blustering when they were halted in front of me, but the captain was awed. There was something about the whole incident that mystified him, and when he got close enough to me to see the color of my hair and eyes, I could see that he was dumfounded.

"This is an outrage," shouted Moosko, the ongyan. "I will see that every last man of you is destroyed for this." He was trembling, and purple with rage.

"See that he does not speak again unless he is spoken to," I instructed Kiron, and then I turned to the captain. "As soon as we have taken what we wish from your ship," I told him, "you will be free to continue your voyage. I am sorry that you did not see fit to obey me when I ordered you to stop for boarding; it would have saved many lives. The next time you are ordered to lay to by the *Sofal,* do so; and when you return to your own country, advise other shipmasters that the *Sofal* is abroad and that she is to be obeyed."

"Do you mind telling me," he asked, "who you are and under what flag you sail?"

"For the moment I am a Vepajan," I replied, "but we sail under our own flag. No country is responsible for what we do, nor are we responsible to any country."

Pressing the crew of the *Yan* into service, Kamlot, Kiron, Gamfor, and Zog had all her weapons, such of her provisions as we wished, and the most valuable and least bulky portion of her cargo transferred to the *Sofal* before dark. We then threw her guns overboard and let her proceed upon her way.

Moosko I retained as a hostage in the event that we should ever need one; he was being held under guard on the main deck until I could determine just what to do with him. The Vepajan women captives we had rescued from the *Sovong,* together with our own officers who were also quartered on the second deck, left me no vacant cabin in which to put Moosko, and I did not wish to confine him below deck in the hole reserved for common prisoners.

I chanced to mention the matter to Kamlot in the presence of Vilor, when the latter immediately suggested that he would share his own small cabin with Moosko and be responsible for him. As this seemed an easy solution of the problem, I ordered Moosko turned over to Vilor, who took him at once to his cabin.

The pursuit of the *Yan* had taken us off our course, and now, as we headed once more toward Vepaja, a dark land mass was dimly visible to starboard. I could not but wonder what mysteries lay beyond that shadowy coast line, what strange beasts and men inhabited that *terra incognita* that stretched away into Strabol and the unexplored equatorial regions of Venus. To partially satisfy my curiosity, I went to the chart room, and after determining our position as accurately as I could by dead reckoning, I discovered that we were off the shore of Noobol. I remembered having heard Danus mention this country, but I could not recall what he had told me about it.

Lured by imaginings, I went out onto the tower deck and stood alone, looking out across the faintly illuminated nocturnal waters of Amtor toward mysterious Noobol. The wind had risen to almost the proportions of a gale, the first that I had encountered since my coming to the Shepherd's Star; heavy seas were commencing to run, but I had every confidence in the ship and in the ability of my officers to navigate her under any circumstances; so I was not perturbed by the increasing violence of the storm. It occurred to me though that the women aboard might be frightened, and my thoughts, which were seldom absent from her for long, returned to Duare. Perhaps she was frightened!

Even no excuse is a good excuse to the man who wishes to see the object of his infatuation; but now I prided myself that I had a real reason for seeing her and one that she herself must appreciate, since it was prompted by solicitude for her welfare. And so I went down the companionway to the second deck with the intention of whistling before the door of Duare; but as I had to pass directly by Vilor's cabin, I thought that I would take the opportunity to look in on my prisoner.

There was a moment's silence following my signal, and then Vilor bade me enter. As I stepped into the cabin, I was surprised to see an angan sitting there with Moosko and Vilor. Vilor's embarrassment was obvious; Moosko appeared ill at ease and the birdman frightened. That they were disconcerted did not surprise me, for it is not customary for members of the superior race to fraternize with klangan socially. But if they were embarrassed, I was not. I was more inclined to be angry. The position of the Vepajans aboard the *Sofal* was a delicate one. We were few in numbers, and our ascendency depended wholly upon the respect we engendered and maintained in the minds of the Thorans, who constituted the majority of our company, and who looked up to the Vepajans as their superiors despite the efforts of their leaders to convince them of the equality of all men.

"Your quarters are forward," I said to the angan; "you do not belong here."

"It is not his fault," said Vilor, as the birdman rose to leave the cabin. "Moosko, strange as it may seem, had never seen an angan; and I fetched this fellow here merely to satisfy his curiosity. I am sorry if I did wrong."

"Of course," I said, "that puts a slightly different aspect on the matter, but I think it will be better if the prisoner inspects the klangan on deck where they belong. He has my permission to do so tomorrow."

The angan departed, I exchanged a few more words with Vilor, and then I left him with his prisoner and turned toward the after cabin where Duare was quartered, the episode that had just occurred fading from my mind almost immediately, to be replaced by far more pleasant thoughts.

There was a light in Duare's cabin as I whistled before her door, wondering if she would invite me in or ignore my presence. For a time there was no response to my signal, and I had about determined that she would not see me, when I heard her soft, low voice inviting me to enter.

"You are persistent," she said, but there was less anger in her voice than when last she had spoken to me.

"I came to ask if the storm has frightened you and to assure you that there is no danger."

"I am not afraid," she replied. "Was that all that you wished to say?"

It sounded very much like a dismissal. "No," I assured her, "nor did I come solely for the purpose of saying it."

She raised her eyebrows. "What else could you have to say to me—that you have not already said?"

"Perhaps I wished to repeat," I suggested.

"You must not!" she cried.

I came closer to her. "Look at me, Duare; look me in the eyes and tell me that you do not like to hear me tell you that I love you!"

Her eyes fell. "I must not listen!" she whispered and rose as though to leave the room.

I was mad with love for her; her near presence sent the hot blood boiling through my veins; I seized her in my arms and drew her to me; before she could prevent it, I covered her lips with mine. Then she partially tore away from me, and I saw a dagger gleaming in her hand.

"You are right," I said. "Strike! I have done an unforgivable thing. My only excuse is my great love for you; it swept away reason and honor."

Her dagger hand dropped to her side. "I cannot," she sobbed, and, turning, fled from the room.

I went back to my own cabin, cursing myself for a beast and a cad. I could not understand how it had been possible for me to have committed such an unpardonable act. I reviled myself, and at the same time the memory of that soft body crushed against mine and those perfect lips against my lips suffused me with a warm glow of contentment that seemed far removed from repentance.

I lay awake for a long time after I went to bed, thinking of Duare, recalling all that had ever passed between us. I found a hidden meaning in her cry, "I must not listen!" I rejoiced in the facts that once she had refused to consign me to death at the hands of others and that again she had refused to kill me herself. Her "I cannot" rang in my ears almost like an avowal of love. My better judgment told that I was quite mad, but I found joy in hugging my madness to me.

The storm increased to such terrific fury during the night that the screeching of the wind and the wild plunging of the *Sofal* awakened me just before dawn. Arising immediately, I went on deck, where the wind almost carried me away. Great waves lifted the *Sofal* on high, only to plunge her the next moment into watery abysses. The ship was pitching violently; occasionally a huge wave broke across her bow and flooded the main deck; across her starboard quarter loomed a great land mass that seemed perilously close. The situation appeared fraught with danger.

I entered the control room and found both Honan and Gamfor with the helmsman. They were worried because of our proximity to land. Should either the engines or the steering device fail, we must inevitably be driven ashore. I told them to remain where they were, and then I went down to the second deck house to arouse Kiron, Kamlot, and Zog.

As I turned aft from the foot of the companionway on the second deck, I noticed that the door of Vilor's cabin was swinging open and closing again with each roll of the vessel; but I gave the matter no particular thought at the time and passed on to awaken my other lieutenants. Having done so, I kept on to Duare's cabin, fearing that, if awake, she might be frightened by the rolling of the ship and the shrieking of the wind. To my surprise, I found her door swinging on its hinges.

Something, I do not know what, aroused my suspicion that all was not right far more definitely than the rather unimportant fact that the door to her outer cabin was unlatched. Stepping quickly inside, I uncovered the light and glanced quickly about the room. There was nothing amiss except, perhaps, the fact that the door to the inner cabin where she slept was also open and swinging on its hinges. I was sure that no one could be sleeping in there while both those doors were swinging and banging. It was possible, of course, that Duare was too frightened to get up and close them.

I stepped to the inner doorway and called her name aloud. There was no reply. I called again, louder; again, silence was my only answer. Now I was definitely perturbed. Stepping into the room, I uncovered the light and looked at the bed. It was empty—Duare was not there! But in the far corner of the cabin lay the body of the man who had stood guard outside her door.

Throwing conventions overboard, I hastened to each of the adjoining cabins where the rest of the Vepajan women were quartered. All were there except Duare. They had not seen her; they did not know where she was. Frantic from apprehension, I ran back to Kamlot's cabin and acquainted him with my tragic discovery. He was stunned.

"She must be on board," he cried. "Where else can she be?"

"I know she *must* be," I replied, "but something tells me she is not. We must search the ship at once—from stem to stern."

Zog and Kiron were emerging from their cabins as I came from Kamlot's. I told them of my discovery and ordered the search commenced; then I hailed a member of the watch and sent him to the crow's nest to question the lookout. I wanted to know whether he had seen anything unusual transpiring on the ship during his watch, for from his lofty perch he could overlook the entire vessel.

"Muster every man," I told Kamlot; "account for every human being on board; search every inch of the ship."

As the men left to obey my instructions, I recalled the coincidence of the two cabin doors swinging wide—Duare's and Vilor's. I could not imagine what relation either fact had to the other, but I was investigating everything, whether it was of a suspicious nature or not; so I ran quickly to Vilor's cabin, and the moment that I uncovered the light I saw that both Vilor and Moosko were missing. But where were they? No man could have left the *Sofal* in that storm and lived, even could he have launched a boat, which would have been impossible of accomplishment, even in fair weather, without detection.

Coming from Vilor's cabin, I summoned a sailor and dispatched him to inform Kamlot that Vilor and Moosko were missing from their cabin and direct him to send them to me as soon as he located them; then I returned to the quarters of the Vepajan women for the purpose of questioning them more carefully.

I was puzzled by the disappearance of Moosko and Vilor, which, taken in conjunction with the absence of Duare from her cabin, constituted a mystery of major proportions; and I was trying to discover some link of circumstance that might point a connection between the two occurrences, when I suddenly recalled Vilor's insistence that he be permitted to guard Duare. Here was the first, faint suggestion of a connecting link. However, it seemed to lead nowhere. These three people had disappeared from their cabins, yet reason assured me that they would be found in a short time, since it was impossible for them to leave the ship, unless——

It was that little word "unless" that terrified me most of all. Since I had discovered that Duare was not in her cabin, a numbing fear had assailed me that, considering herself dishonored by my avowal of love, she had hurled herself overboard. Of what value now the fact that I constantly upbraided myself for my lack of consideration and control? Of what weight my vain regrets?

Yet now I saw a tiny ray of hope. If the absence of Vilor and Moosko from their cabin and Duare from hers were more than a coincidence, then it were safe to assume that they were together and ridiculous to believe that all three had leaped overboard.

With these conflicting fears and hopes whirling through my brain, I came to the quarters of the Vepajan women, which I was about to enter when the sailor I had sent to question the lookout in the crow's nest came running toward me in a state of evident excitement.

"Well," I demanded, as, breathless, he halted before me, "what did the lookout have to say?"

"Nothing, my captain," replied the man, his speech retarded by excitement and exertion.

"Nothing! and why not?" I snapped.

"The lookout is dead, my captain," gasped the sailor.

"Dead!"

"Murdered."

"How?" I asked.

"A sword had been run through his body—from behind, I think. He lay upon his face."

"Go at once and inform Kamlot; tell him to replace the lookout and investigate his death, then to report to me."

Shaken by this ominous news, I entered the quarters of the women. They were huddled together in one cabin, pale and frightened, but outwardly calm.

"Have you found Duare?" one of them asked immediately.

"No," I replied, "but I have discovered another mystery—the ongyan, Moosko, is missing and with him the Vepajan, Vilor."

"Vepajan!" exclaimed Byea, the woman who had questioned me concerning Duare. "Vilor is no Vepajan."

"What do you mean?" I demanded. "If he is not a Vepajan, what is he?"

"He is a Thoran spy," she replied. "He was sent to Vepaja long ago to steal the secret of the longevity serum, and when we were captured the klangan took him, also, by mistake. We learned this, little by little, aboard the *Sovong*."

"But why was I not informed when he was brought aboard?" I demanded.

"We supposed that everyone knew it," explained Byea, "and thought that Vilor was transferred to the *Sofal* as a prisoner."

Another link in the chain of accumulating evidence! Yet I was as far as ever from knowing where either end of the chain lay.

CHAPTER FOURTEEN

Storm

After questioning the women, I went to the main deck, too impatient to await the reports of my lieutenants in the tower where I belonged. I found that they had searched the ship and were just coming to me with their report. None of those previously discovered missing had been found, but the search had revealed another astounding fact—the five klangan also were missing!

Searching certain portions of the ship had been rather dangerous work, as she was rolling heavily, and the deck was still occasionally swept by the larger seas; but it had been accomplished without mishap, and the men were now congregated in a large room in the main deck house. Kamlot, Gamfor, Kiron, Zog, and I had also entered this same room, where we were discussing the whole mysterious affair. Honan was in the control room of the tower.

I told them that I had just discovered that Vilor was not Vepajan but a Thoran spy, and had reminded Kamlot of the man's request that he be allowed to guard the janjong. "I learned something else from Byea while I was questioning the women, I added. "During their captivity aboard the *Sovong,* Vilor persisted in annoying Duare with his attentions; he was infatuated with her."

"I think that gives us the last bit of evidence we need to enable us to reconstruct the hitherto seemingly inexplicable happenings of the past night," said Gamfor. "Vilor wished to possess Duare; Moosko wished to escape from captivity. The former had fraternized with the klangan and made friends of them; that was known to everyone aboard the *Sofal.* Moosko was an ongyan; during all their lives, doubtless, the klangan have looked upon the klongyan as the fountain heads of supreme authority. They would believe his promises, and they would obey his commands.

"Doubtless Vilor and Moosko worked out the details of the plot together. They dispatched an angan to kill the lookout, lest their movements arouse suspicion and be reported before they could carry their plan to a successful conclusion. The lookout disposed of, the other klangan congregated in Vilor's cabin; then Vilor, probably accompanied by Moosko, went to the cabin of Duare, where they killed the guard and seized her in her sleep, silenced her with a gag, and carried her to the gangway outside, where the klangan were waiting.

"A gale was blowing, it is true, but it was blowing toward land which lay but a short distance to starboard; and the klangan are powerful fliers.

"There you have what I believe to be a true picture of what happened aboard the *Sofal* while we slept."

"And you believe that the klangan carried these three people to the shores of Noobol?" I asked.

"I think there can be no question but that such is the fact," replied Gamfor.

"I quite agree with him," interjected Kamlot.

"Then there is but one thing to do," I announced. "We must turn back and land a searching party on Noobol."

"No boat could live in this sea," objected Kiron.

"The storm will not last forever," I reminded him. "We shall lie off the shore until it abates. I am going up to the tower; I wish you men would remain here and question the crew; it is possible that there may be some one among them who has overheard something that will cast new light on the subject. The klangan are great talkers, and they may have dropped some remark that will suggest the ultimate destination Vilor and Moosko had in mind."

As I stepped out onto the main deck, the *Sofal* rose upon the crest of a great wave and then plunged nose downward into the watery abyss beyond, tilting the deck forward at an angle of almost forty-five degrees. The wet and slippery boards beneath my feet gave them no hold, and I slid helplessly forward almost fifty feet before I could check my descent. Then the ship buried her nose in a mountainous wave and a great wall of water swept the deck from stem to stern, picking me up and whirling me helplessly upon its crest.

For a moment I was submerged, and then a vagary of the Titan that had seized me brought my head above the water, and I saw the *Sofal* rolling and pitching fifty feet away.

Even in the immensity of interstellar space I had never felt more helpless nor more hopeless than I did at that moment on the storm-lashed sea of an unknown world, surrounded by darkness and chaos and what terrible creatures of this mysterious deep I could not even guess. I was lost! Even if my comrades knew of the disaster that had overwhelmed me, they were helpless to give me aid. No boat could live in that sea, as Kiron had truly reminded us, and no swimmer could breast the terrific onslaught of those racing, wind-driven mountains of water that might no longer be described by so puny a word as wave.

Hopeless! I should not have said that; I am never without hope. If I could not swim against the sea, perhaps I might swim with it; and at no great distance lay land. I am an experienced distance swimmer and a powerful man. If any man could survive in such a sea, I knew that I could; but if I could not, I was determined that I should at least have the satisfaction of dying fighting.

I was hampered by no clothes, as one could scarcely dignify the Amtorian loincloth with the name of clothing; my only impediment was my weapons; and these I hesitated to discard, knowing that my chances for survival on that unfriendly shore would be slight were I unarmed. Neither the belt, nor the pistol, nor the dagger inconvenienced me, and their weight was negligible; but the sword was a different matter. If you have never tried swimming with a sword dangling from your middle, do not attempt it in a heavy sea. You might think that it would hang straight down and not get in the way, but mine did not. The great waves hurled me about mercilessly, twisting and turning me; and now my sword was buffeting me in some tender spot, and now it was getting between my legs, and once, when a wave turned me completely over, it came down on top of me and struck me on the head; yet I would not discard it.

After the first few minutes of battling with the sea, I concluded that I was in no immediate danger of being drowned. I could keep my head above the waves often enough and long enough to insure sufficient air for my lungs; and, the water being warm, I was in no danger of being chilled to exhaustion, as so often occurs when men are thrown into cold seas. Therefore, as closely as I could anticipate any contingency in this unfamiliar world, there remained but two major and immediate threats against my life. The first lay in the possibility of attack by some ferocious monster of the Amtorian deeps; the second, and by far the more serious, the storm-lashed shore upon which I must presently attempt to make a safe landing.

This in itself should have been sufficient to dishearten me, for I had seen seas breaking upon too many shores to lightly ignore the menace of those incalculable tons of hurtling waters pounding, crashing, crushing, tearing their way even into the rocky heart of the eternal hills.

I swam slowly in the direction of the shore, which, fortunately for me, was in the direction that the storm was carrying me. I had no mind to sap my strength by unnecessarily overexerting myself; and so, as I took it easily, content to keep afloat as I moved slowly shoreward, daylight came; and as each succeeding wave lifted me to its summit, I saw the shore with increasing clearness. It lay about a mile from me, and its aspect was most forbidding. Huge combers were breaking upon a rocky coast line, throwing boiling fountains of white spume high in air; above the howling of the tempest, the thunder of the surf rolled menacingly across that mile of angry sea to warn me that death lay waiting to embrace me at the threshold of safety.

I was in a quandary. Death lay all about me; it remained but for me to choose the place and manner of the assignation; I could drown where I was, or I could permit myself to be dashed to pieces on the rocks. Neither eventuality aroused any considerable enthusiasm in my breast. As a mistress, death seemed sadly lacking in many essentials. Therefore, I decided not to die.

Thoughts may be, as has been said, things; but they are not everything. No matter how favorably I thought of living, I knew that I must also do something about it. My present situation offered me no chance of salvation; the shore alone could give me life; so I struck out for the shore. As I drew nearer it, many things, some of them quite irrelevant, passed through my mind; but some were relevant, among them the Burial Service. It was not a nice time to think of this, but then we cannot always control our thoughts; however, "In the midst of life we are in death" seemed wholly appropriate to my situation. By twisting it a bit, I achieved something that contained the germ of hope—in the midst of death there is life. Perhaps——

The tall waves, lifting me high, afforded me for brief instants vantage points from which I could view the death ahead in the midst of which I sought for life. The shore line was becoming, at closer range, something more than an unbroken line of jagged rocks and white water; but details were yet lacking, for each time I was allowed but a brief glimpse before being dropped once more to the bottom of a watery chasm.

My own efforts, coupled with the fury of the gale driving me shoreward, brought me rapidly to the point where I should presently be seized by the infuriated seas and hurled upon the bombarded rocks that reared their jagged heads bleakly above the swirling waters of each receding comber.

A great wave lifted me upon its crest and carried me forward—the end had come! With the speed of a race horse it swept me toward my doom; a welter of spume engulfed my head; I was twisted and turned as a cork in a whirlpool; yet I struggled to lift my mouth above the surface for an occasional gasp of air; I fought to live for a brief moment longer, that I might not be dead when I was dashed by the merciless sea against the merciless rocks—thus dominating is the urge to live.

I was carried on; moments seemed an eternity! Where were the rocks? I almost yearned for them now to end the bitterness of my futile struggle. I thought of my mother and of Duare. I even contemplated, with something akin to philosophic calm, the strangeness of my end. In that other world that I had left forever no creature would ever have knowledge of my fate. Thus spoke the eternal egotism of man, who, even in death, desires an audience.

Now I caught a brief glimpse of rocks. They were upon my left! when they should have been in front of me. It was incomprehensible.

The wave tore on, carrying me with it; and still I lived, and there was only water against my naked flesh.

Now the fury of the sea abated. I rose to the crest of a diminishing comber to look with astonishment upon the comparatively still waters of an inlet. I had been carried through the rocky gateway of a landlocked cove, and before me I saw a sandy crescent beach. I had escaped the black fingers of death; I had been the beneficiary of a miracle!

The sea gave me a final flip that rolled me high upon the sands to mingle with the wrack and flotsam she had discarded. I stood up and looked about me. A more devout man would have given thanks, but I felt that as yet I had little for which to give thanks. My life had been spared temporarily, but Duare was still in peril.

The cove into which I had been swept was formed by the mouth of a canyon that ran inland between low hills, the sides and summits of which were dotted with small trees. Nowhere did I see any such giants as grow in Vepaja; but perhaps, I mused, what I see here are not trees on Venus but only underbrush. However, I shall call them trees, since many of them were from fifty to eighty feet in height.

A little river tumbled down the canyon's bottom to empty into the cove; pale violet grass, starred with blue and purple flowers, bordered it and clothed the hills. There were trees with red boles, smooth and glossy as lacquer. There were trees with azure boles. Whipping in the gale was the same weird foliage of heliotrope and lavender and violet that had rendered the forests of Vepaja so unearthly to my eyes. But beautiful and unusual as was the scene, it could not claim my undivided attention. A strange freak of fate had thrown me upon this shore to which, I had reason to believe, Duare must undoubtedly have been carried; and now my only thought was to take advantage of this fortunate circumstance and attempt to find and succor her.

I could only assume that in the event her abductors had brought her to this shore their landing must have been made farther along the coast to my right, which was the direction from which the *Sofal* had been moving. With only this slight and unsatisfactory clue, I started immediately to scale the side of the canyon and commence my search.

At the summit I paused a moment to survey the surrounding country and get my bearings. Before me stretched a rolling table-land, tree-dotted and lush with grass, and beyond that, inland, rose a range of mountains, vague and mysterious along the distant horizon. My course lay to the east, along the coast (I shall use the earthly references to points of compass); the mountains were northward, toward the equator. I am assuming of course that I am in the southern hemisphere of the planet. The sea was south of me. I glanced in that direction, looking for the *Sofal*; there she was, far out and moving toward the east. Evidently my orders were being carried out, and the *Sofal* was lying off shore waiting for calm weather that would permit a landing.

Now I turned my steps toward the east. At each elevation I stopped and scanned the table-land in all directions, searching for some sign of those I sought. I saw signs of life, but not of human life. Herbivorous animals grazed in large numbers upon the flower-starred violet plain. Many that were close enough to be seen plainly appeared similar in form to earthly animals, but there was none exactly like anything I had ever seen on earth. Their extreme wariness and the suggestion of speed and agility in their conformations suggested that they had enemies; the wariness, that among these enemies was man; the speed and agility, that swift and ferocious carnivores preyed upon them.

These observations served to warn me that I must be constantly on the alert for similar dangers that might threaten me, and I was glad that the table-land was well supplied with trees growing at convenient intervals. I had not forgotten the ferocious basto that Kamlot and I had encountered in Vepaja, and, though I had seen nothing quite so formidable as yet among the nearer beasts, there were some creatures grazing at a considerable distance from me whose lines suggested a too great similarity to those bisonlike omnivores to insure ease of mind.

I moved rather rapidly, as I was beset by fears for Duare's safety and felt that if I did not come upon some clue this first day my search might prove fruitless. The klangan, it believed, must have alighted near the coast, where they would have remained at least until daylight, and my hope was that they might have tarried longer. If they had winged away immediately, my chances of locating them were slight; and now my only hope lay in the slender possibility that I might come across them before they took up their flight for the day.

The table-land was cut by gullies and ravines running down to the sea. Nearly all of these carried streams varying in size from tiny rivulets to those which might be dignified by the appellation of river, but none that I encountered offered any serious obstacle to my advance, though upon one or two occasions I was forced to swim the deeper channels. If these rivers were inhabited by dangerous reptiles, I saw nothing of them, though I admit that they were constantly on my mind as I made my way from bank to bank.

Once, upon the table-land, I saw a large, catlike creature at a distance, apparently stalking a herd of what appeared to be a species of antelope; but either it did not see me or was more interested in its natural prey, for although I was in plain sight, it paid no attention to me.

Shortly thereafter I dropped into a small gully, and when I had regained the higher ground upon the opposite side the beast was no longer in sight; but even had it been, it would have been driven from my thoughts by faint sounds that came to me out of the distance far ahead. There were what sounded like the shouts of men and the unmistakable hum of Amtorian pistol fire.

Though I searched diligently with my eyes to the far horizon, I could see no sign of the authors of these noises; but it was enough for me to know that there were human beings ahead and that there was fighting there. Being only human, I naturally pictured the woman I loved in the center of overwhelming dangers, even though my better judgment told me that the encounter reverberating in the distance might have no connection with her or her abductors.

Reason aside, however, I broke into a run; and as I advanced the sounds waxed louder. They led me finally to the rim of a considerable canyon, the bottom of which formed a level valley of entrancing loveliness, through which wound a river far larger than any I had yet encountered.

But neither the beauty of the valley nor the magnitude of the river held my attention for but an instant. Down there upon the floor of that nameless canyon was a scene that gripped my undivided interest and left me cold with apprehension. Partially protected by an outcropping of rock at the river's edge, six figures crouched or lay. Five of them were klangan, the sixth a woman. It was Duare!

Facing them, hiding behind trees and rocks, were a dozen hairy, manlike creatures hurling rocks from slings at the beleaguered six or loosing crude arrows from still cruder bows. The savages and the klangan were hurling taunts and insults at one another, as well as missiles; it was these sounds that I had heard from a distance blending with the staccato hum of the klangan's pistols.

Three of the klangan lay motionless upon the turf behind their barrier, apparently dead. The remaining klangan and Duare crouched with pistols in their hands, defending their position and their lives. The savages cast their stone missiles directly at the three whenever one of them showed any part of his body above the rocky breastwork, but the arrows they discharged into the air so that they fell behind the barrier.

Scattered about among the trees and behind rocks were the bodies of fully a dozen hairy savages who had fallen before the fire of the klangan, but, while Duare's defenders had taken heavy toll of the enemy, the outcome of the unequal battle could have been only the total destruction of the klangan and Duare had it lasted much longer.

The details which have taken long in the telling I took in at a single glance, nor did I waste precious time in pondering the best course of action. At any moment one of those crude arrows might pierce the girl I loved; and so my first thought was to divert the attention of the savages, and perhaps their fire, from their intended victims to me.

I was slightly behind their position, which gave me an advantage, as also did the fact that I was above them. Yelling like a Comanche, I leaped down the steep side of the canyon, firing my pistol as I charged. Instantly the scene below me changed. The savages, taken partially from the rear and unexpectedly menaced by a new enemy, leaped to their feet in momentary bewilderment; and simultaneously the two remaining klangan, recognizing me and realizing that succor was at hand, sprang from the shelter of their barrier and ran forward to complete the demoralization of the savages.

Together we shot down six of the enemy before the rest finally turned and fled, but they were not routed before one of the klangan was struck full between the eyes by a jagged bit of rock. I saw him fall, and when we were no longer menaced by a foe I went to him, thinking that he was only stunned; but at that time I had no conception of the force with which these primitive, apelike men cast the missiles from their slings. The fellow's skull was crushed, and a portion of the missile had punctured his brain. He was quite dead when I reached him.

Then I hastened to Duare. She was standing with a pistol in her hand, tired and dishevelled, but otherwise apparently little worse for the harrowing experiences through which she had passed. I think that she was glad to see me, for she certainly must have preferred me to the hairy apemen from which I had been instrumental in rescuing her; yet a trace of fear was reflected in her eyes, as though she were not quite sure of the nature of the treatment she might expect from me. To my shame, her fears were justified by my past behavior; but I was determined that she should never again have cause to complain of me. I would win her confidence and trust, hoping that love might follow in their wake.

There was no light of welcome in her eyes as I approached her, and that hurt me more than I can express. Her countenance reflected more a pathetic resignation to whatever new trials my presence might portend.

"You have not been harmed?" I asked. "You are all right?"

"Quite," she replied. Her eyes passed beyond me, searching the summit of the canyon wall down which I had charged upon the savages. "Where are the others?" she asked in puzzled and slightly troubled tones.

"What others?" I inquired.

"Those who came with you from the *Sofal* to search for me."

"There were no others; I am quite alone."

Her countenance assumed an even deeper gloom at this announcement. "Why did you come alone?" she asked fearfully.

"To be honest with you, it was through no fault of my own that I came at all at this time," I explained. "After we missed you from the *Sofal,* I gave orders to stand by off the coast until the storm abated and we could land a searching party. Immediately thereafter I was swept overboard, a most fortunate circumstance as it turned out; and naturally when I found myself safely ashore my first thought was of you. I was searching for you when I heard the shouts of the savages and the sound of pistol fire."

"You came in time to save me from them," she said, "but for what? What are you going to do with me now?"

"I am going to take you to the coast as quickly as possible," I replied, "and there we will signal the *Sofal.* She will send a boat to take us off."

Duare appeared slightly relieved at this recital of my plans. "You will win the undying gratitude of the jong, my father, if you return me to Vepaja unharmed," she said.

"To have served his daughter shall be reward enough for me," I replied, "even though I succeed in winning not even her gratitude."

"That you already have for what you have just done at the risk of your life," she assured me, and there was more graciousness in her voice than before.

"What became of Vilor and Moosko?" I asked.

Her lip curled in scorn. "When the kloonobargan attacked us, they fled."

"Where did they go?" I asked.

"They swam the river and ran away in that direction." She pointed toward the east.

"Why did the klangan not desert you also?"

"They were told to protect me. They know little else than to obey their superiors, and, too, they like to fight. Having little intelligence and no imagination, they are splendid fighters."

"I cannot understand why they did not fly away from danger and take you with them when they saw that defeat was certain. That would have insured the safety of all."

"By the time they were assured of that, it was too late," she explained. "They could not have risen from behind our protection without being destroyed by the missiles of the kloonobargan."

This word, by way of parenthesis, is an interesting example of the derivation of an Amtorian substantive. Broadly, it means savages; literally, it means hairy men. In the singular, it is nobargan. *Gan* is man; *bar* is hair. No is a contraction of *not* (with), and is used as a prefix with the same value that the suffix *y* has in English; therefore *nobar* means hairy, *nobargan,* hairy man. The prefix *kloo* forms the plural, and we have *kloonobargan* (hairy men), savages.

After determining that the four klangan were dead, Duare, the remaining angan, and I started down the river toward the ocean. On the way Duare told me what had occurred on board the *Sofal* the preceding night, and I discovered that it had been almost precisely as Gamfor had pictured it.

"What was their object in taking you with them?" I asked.

"Vilor wanted me," she replied.

"And Moosko merely wished to escape?"

"Yes. He thought that he would be killed when the ship reached Vepaja."

"How did they expect to survive in a wild country like this?" I asked. "Did they know where they were?"

"They said that they thought that the country was Noobol," she replied, "but they were not positive. The Thorans have agents in Noobol who are fomenting discord in an attempt to overthrow the government. There are several of these in a city on the coast, and it was Moosko's intention to search for this city, where he was certain that he would find friends who would be able to arrange transportation for himself, Vilor, and me to Thora."

We walked on in silence for some time. I was just ahead of Duare, and the angan brought up the rear. He was crestfallen and dejected. His head and tail feathers drooped. The klangan are ordinarily so vociferous that this preternatural silence attracted my attention, and, thinking that he might have been injured in the fight, I questioned him.

"I was not wounded, my captain," he replied.

"Then what is the matter with you? Are you sad because of the deaths of your comrades?"

"It is not that," he replied; "there are plenty more where they came from. It is because of my own death that I am sad."

"But you are not dead!"

"I shall be soon," he averred.

"What makes you think so?" I demanded.

"When I return to the ship, they will kill me for what I did last night. If I do not return, I shall be killed here. No one could live alone for long in such a country as this."

"If you serve me well and obey me, you will not be killed if we succeed in reaching the *Sofal* again," I assured him.

At that he brightened perceptibly. "I shall serve you well and obey you, my captain," he promised, and presently he was smiling and singing again as though he had not a single care in the world and there was no such thing as death.

On several occasions, when I had glanced back at my companions, I had discovered Duare's eyes upon me, and in each instance she had turned them away quickly, as though I had surprised and embarrassed her in some questionable act. I had spoken to her only when necessary, for I had determined to atone for my previous conduct by maintaining a purely official attitude toward her that would reassure her and give her no cause for apprehension as to my intentions.

This was a difficult rôle for me to play while I yearned to take her into my arms and tell her again of the great love that was consuming me; but I had succeeded so far in controlling myself and saw no reason to believe that I should not be able to continue to do so, at least as long as Duare continued to give me no encouragement. The very idea that she might give me encouragement caused me to smile in spite of myself.

Presently, much to my surprise, she said, "You are very quiet. What is the matter?"

It was the first time that Duare had ever opened a conversation with me or given me any reason to believe that I existed for her as a personality; I might have been a clod of earth or a piece of furniture, for all the interest she had seemed to take in me since those two occasions upon which I had surprised her as she watched me from the concealing foliage of her garden.

"There is nothing the matter with me," I assured her. "I am only concerned with your welfare and the necessity for getting you back to the *Sofal* as quickly as possible."

"You do not talk any more," she complained. "Formerly, when I saw you, you used to talk a great deal."

"Probably altogether too much," I admitted, "but you see, now I am trying not to annoy you."

Her eyes fell to the ground. "It would not annoy me," she said almost inaudibly, but now that I was invited to do the very thing that I had been longing to do, I became dumb; I could think of nothing to say. "You see," she continued in her normal voice, "conditions are very different now from any that I have ever before encountered. The rules and restrictions under which I have lived among my own people cannot, I now realize, be expected to apply to situations so unusual or to people and places so foreign to those whose lives they were intended to govern.

"I have been thinking a great deal about many things—and you. I commenced to think these strange thoughts after I saw you the first time in the garden at Kooaad. I have thought that perhaps it might be nice to talk to other men than those I am permitted to see in the house of my father, the jong. I became tired of talking to these same men and to my women, but custom had made a slave and a coward of me. I did not dare do the things I most wished to do. I always wanted to talk to you, and now for the brief time before we shall be again aboard the *Sofal,* where I must again be governed by the laws of Vepaja, I am going to be free; I am going to do what I wish; I am going to talk to you."

This naïve declaration revealed a new Duare, one in the presence of whom it was going to be most difficult to maintain an austere Platonicism; yet I continued to steel myself to the carrying out of my resolve.

"Why do you not talk to me?" she demanded when I made no immediate comment on her confession.

"I do not know what to talk about," I admitted, "unless I talk about the one thing that is uppermost in my mind."

She was silent for a moment, her brows knit in thought, and then she asked with seeming innocence, "What is that?"

"Love," I said, looking into her eyes.

Her lids dropped and her lips trembled. "No!" she exclaimed. "We must not talk of that; it is wrong; it is wicked."

"Is love wicked on Amtor?" I asked.

"No, no; I do not mean that," she hastened to deny; "but it is wrong to speak to me of love until after I am twenty."

"May I then, Duare?" I asked.

She shook her head, a little sadly I thought. "No, not even then," she answered. "You may never speak to me of love, without sinning, nor may I listen without sinning, for I am the daughter of a jong."

"Perhaps it would be safer were we not to talk at all," I said glumly.

"Oh, yes, let us talk," she begged. "Tell me about the strange world you are supposed to come from."

To amuse her, I did as she requested; and walking beside her I devoured her with my eyes until at last we came to the ocean. Far out I saw the *Sofal,* and now came the necessity for devising a scheme by which we might signal her.

On either side of the canyon, through which the river emptied into the ocean, were lofty cliffs. That on the west side, and nearer us, was the higher, and to this I made my way, accompanied by Duare and the angan. The ascent was steep, and most of the way I found it, or made it, necessary to assist Duare, so that often I had my arm about her as I half carried her upward.

At first I feared that she might object to this close contact; but she did not, and in some places where it was quite level and she needed no help, though I still kept my arm about her, she did not draw away nor seem to resent the familiarity.

At the summit of the cliff I hastily gathered dead wood and leaves with the assistance of the angan, and presently we had a signal fire sending a smoke column into the air. The wind had abated, and the smoke rose far above the cliff before it was dissipated. I was positive that it would be seen aboard the *Sofal,* but whether it would be correctly interpreted, I could not know.

A high sea was still running that would have precluded the landing of a small boat, but we had the angan, and if the *Sofal* were to draw in more closely to shore, he could easily transport us to her deck one at a time. However, I hesitated to risk Duare in the attempt while the ship was at its present considerable distance from shore, as what wind there was would have been directly in the face of the angan.

From the summit of this cliff we could overlook the cliff on the east side of the canyon, and presently the angan called my attention to something in that direction. "Men are coming," he said.

I saw them immediately, but they were still too far away for me to be able to identify them, though even at a distance I was sure that they were not of the same race as the savages which had attacked Duare and the klangan.

Now indeed it became imperative that we attract the attention of the *Sofal* immediately, and to that end I built two more fires at intervals from the first, so that it might be obvious to anyone aboard the ship that this was in fact a signal rather than an accidental fire or a camp fire.

Whether or not the *Sofal* had seen our signal, it was evident that the party of men approaching must have; and I could not but believe that, attracted by it, they were coming to investigate. Constantly they were drawing nearer, and as the minutes passed we saw that they were armed men of the same race as the Vepajans.

They were still some distance away when we saw the *Sofal* change her course and point her bow toward shore. Our signal had been seen, and our comrades were coming to investigate; but would they be in time? For us it was a thrilling race. The wind had sprung up again and the sea was rising once more. I asked the angan if he could breast the gale, for I had determined to send Duare off at once if I received a favorable reply.

"I could alone," he said, "but I doubt that I could if I were carrying another."

We watched the *Sofal* plunging and wallowing in the rising sea as it forged steadily closer, and we watched the men drawing near with equal certainty. There was no doubt in my mind as to which would reach us first; my only hope now was that the *Sofal* could lessen the distance in the meantime sufficiently so that it would be safe for the angan to attempt to carry Duare to her.

Now the men had reached the summit of the cliff on the opposite side of the canyon, and here they halted and observed us while carrying on a discussion of some nature.

"Vilor is with them!" exclaimed Duare suddenly.

"And Moosko," I added. "I see them both now."

"What shall we do?" cried Duare. "Oh, they must not get me again!"

"They shall not," I promised her.

Down the canyon side they came now. We watched them swim the river and cross to the foot of the cliff where we were standing. We watched the *Sofal* creeping slowly shoreward. I went to the edge of the cliff and looked down upon the ascending men. They were half way up now. Then I returned to Duare and the angan.

"We can wait no longer," I said, and then to the angan, "Take the janjong and fly to the ship. She is closer now; you can make it; you *must* make it!"

He started to obey, but Duare drew away from him. "I will not go," she said quietly. "I will not leave you here alone!"

For those words I would gladly have laid down my life. Here again was still another Duare. I had expected nothing like this, for I did not feel that she owed me any such loyalty. It was not as though she had loved me; one might expect such self-sacrifice on the part of a woman for the man she loves. I was swept completely from my feet, but only for an instant. The enemy, if such it were, must by now be almost to the summit of the cliff, in a moment they would be upon us, and even as the thought touched my mind, I saw the first of them running toward us.

"Take her!" I cried to the angan. "There is no time to waste now."

He reached for her, but she attempted to elude him; and then I caught her, and as I touched her, all my good resolutions were swept away, as I felt her in my arms. I pressed her to me for an instant; I kissed her, and then I gave her over to the birdman.

"Hurry!" I cried. "They come!"

Spreading his powerful wings, he rose from the ground, while Duare stretched her hands toward me. "Do not send me away from you, Carson! Do not send me away! I love you!"

But it was too late; I would not have called her back could I have done so, for the armed men were upon me.

Thus I went into captivity in the land of Noobol, an adventure that is no part of this story; but I went with the knowledge that the woman I loved, loved me, and I was happy.

THE END

PHILLIP R. BURGER

In Defense of Carson Napier

In the pantheon of Burroughs heroes, Carson Napier is considered a tad deficient.

He's a poor copy of John Carter of Mars, an incompetent boob, an accident waiting to happen, a dolt, a dullard, a dim bulb. He's cautious to the point of cowardice, he's unsure of his own abilities, and he can't even aim his spaceship in the right direction. In short, he's a complete and utter washout.

Burroughs readers are accustomed to seeing their favorite author and his creations treated with such contempt. The strange thing is Burroughs readers themselves have made this assessment of Carson Napier. Self-professed "True Fans"—those who wrap their lives around Burroughs's writings in the way Trekkers worship the words of Mr. Spock—can't stand ol' Wrong Way Carson.

That's just fine. When I was thirteen I didn't think much of Carson either. He didn't have John Carter's fighting abilities, David Innes of Pellucidar's neocolonial ambitions, or Tarzan's nasty attitude. Burroughs's vision of Venus—Amtor to its inhabitants—just didn't seem exciting enough (maybe because it was always cloudy) and couldn't hold a candle to the fantasy Mars he named Barsoom. But then I grew up and eventually realized that Burroughs as a writer had grown up as well, or at least was trying to. Written in 1931, twenty years into his career, *Pirates of Venus* was Burroughs's attempt to breathe some life into a well-worn field, an attempt to make his rather simple brand of science fiction relevant again. Flawed and incompetent characters peopled mainstream fiction, so Burroughs gave a nod to current literary trends with Carson Napier. At least that is one way this former thirteen-year-old justifies his adult enjoyment of Burroughs's Venus epic. As for the True Fans—well, they will always have Barsoom.

Really, in a side-by-side comparison with Burroughs's other heroes, Carson doesn't come out all that bad. Sure, he and his top-flight team of scientists neglected the moon in their orbital calculations, but that's an honest blunder compared to the blind spots of other Burroughs heroes. For instance: David Innes mistakes a giant winged reptile wrapped in a lion skin for his buxom cave girlfriend; John Carter can never remember how many days there are in a year; Tarzan fights off the barbaric charms of La of Opar, even when he has amnesia, has lost all civilized inhibitions, and can't remember his beloved Jane. Sure, Burroughs had to abide by the strict moral code of his day, but even as a thirteen-year-old I thought the ape-man's steely reserve in this instance a bit of a stretch. Or perhaps this merely speaks of a youthful preference for La over the fairly bland Jane.

No, Carson isn't cut from the same cloth as Burroughs's other heroes, thank goodness. When Carson lands on Venus sans weapons he sensibly concludes that he "could not hope, single-handed, to conquer a world"—Burroughs's way of informing the reader that Carson Napier is no John Carter. Truth be told, Carson's humble opinion of his talents is a pleasant alternative to John Carter's insufferable braggadocio. When the self-professed "greatest swordsman of two worlds" tells a defeated opponent that "it were no disgrace to be bested by John Carter," you rather wish some skulking enemy would creep up behind him and whack Carter on the noggin. Luckily, Burroughs rarely disappoints in this regard.

As for Carson's whole "aimed for Mars but landed on Venus" problem, remember this: dozens upon dozens of otherwise brilliant NASA scientists keep losing satellites they lob toward the Red Planet. In Carson's defense, he discovered his error right away and didn't spend any taxpayer money in his endeavor.

Yes, in spite of his shortcomings (or because of them) I like Carson Napier. I've become rather fond of *Pirates of Venus* as well, in spite of the novel's rather glaring fault: no plot. In fact, the same can be said of the entire Venus series. In the second book Carson and his lady-love, Duare, are *Lost on Venus*—which pretty much sums up the plot. Later on they make their *Escape on Venus*—which pretty much sums up the plot. No major villain appears with whom the hero does battle (Moosko the Ongyan is introduced late in the first book and abandoned rather quickly in the second). Creatures and creations like the klangan are brought in to move the story along and then shuffled off the stage. Characters like Carson's good friend Kamlot and the pirates of *Pirates* are introduced and then dropped. With a topsy-turvy sense of geography countries are very much isolated and have little social intercourse. Amtor has no geopolitical unity and so doesn't seem to be a cohesive creation, which only exacerbates the series' lack of direction.

Burroughs's novels are tales of discovery, wherein the hero finds himself in a previously unknown world and spends a great deal of time and energy battling hostile flora and fauna while he sees the sights. But in addition to rescuing the princess and winning her love, Burroughs gives his heroes some kind of goal: David Innes must free the humans of Pellucidar from their reptilian overlords; John Carter must free the city-state of Helium from its besiegers. By the time Carson Napier becomes one of the titular pirates of Venus, Burroughs should have come up with *something* resembling a plot. All Carson expresses an interest in doing is traveling about to visit the many lands of Amtor. Burroughs obliges, with a new city or country introduced every few chapters but little to connect it with the previously visited city or country.

If John Carter had been in Carson's sandals he would have vowed to overthrow the upstart Thorist government and restore the Vepajan monarchy. Carson doesn't come anywhere near Thora; the most he hopes to accomplish is restoring Duare to her father, she being the sole heir to the Vepajan throne and "the hope of a world." When this goal is reached at the conclusion of *Carson of Venus*, the loving couple reconciles their personal feelings with their societal obligations by hightailing it out of Vepaja, thereby ensuring the dynasty's extinction and the eventual collapse of Vepajan society. We are a long way from the morally righteous John Carter and his duty-bound Martians!

What a difference twenty years makes. When Burroughs first breathed life into John Carter and Tarzan back in 1911, Americans were confident about their place in the world. The country had become an economic Juggernaut, had recently "liberated" several overseas territories (while staying to govern the locals until such time as they could govern themselves), and was above the petty disagreements of the European community. Such brash Americanness can be found in Burroughs's early fiction, wherein a modern civilized man in a primitive land battles and wins against overwhelming odds; the simple natives then recognize the hero's superiority and make him their leader. Our hero sets up an empire, combining civilized skills with primitive virtues under a sort of benign dictatorship. Peace reigns and everybody has what they want—until the sequel.

Fast forward to 1931, and things are very different. The Great Depression is in full swing, the foundation of society appears to be crumbling, and no one seems to have learned anything from the Great War. The benign dictators of Europe, who offered to solve all their followers' problems, proved to be anything but benign, which in time would lead the world to an even more calamitous war. With the world in a such a state of economic and political turmoil, Burroughs may have felt that another godlike hero who becomes the savior of a planet would be out of fashion. Carson has no desire to carve out an empire in the howling wilderness, nor is Amtor a world for the taking; no one can find their way around the place, even when they divide everything by the square root of minus one.

Changes in Burroughs's personal life ought to be considered too. Back in 1911 he discovered his calling as a writer; more important was the knowledge that he would be able to properly support his young wife and their two children (soon to be three). By 1931 Burroughs's marriage was almost at an end; in a few years he would marry another woman, a family friend half his age, forming a relationship that would strain his ties with his children. The old sense of duty and loyalty had to give way to Burroughs's more personal interests. The newly married couple would eventually move to Hawaii, where Burroughs would maintain a heavy social calendar in order to appear youthful to his young bride. The couple would never stay at any one address for long, until this marriage too ended.

Now consider Carson. He is love struck with a girl ten years his junior—much is made of the fact that she is under legal age (by Amtorian standards) and quite virginal. They travel from place to place, the action and pacing of the novels resembling a Saturday matinée serial. A similar criticism can be made of the later Tarzan and Pellucidar books as well. But what keeps the Venus series interesting and compensates for its general lack of direction, at least in the first three books, is watching how Carson and Duare work out their romantic problems. Their course to true love is probably the most torturous in the entire Burroughs canon. Burroughs seems genuinely interested in making Duare more than just a kidnap victim. While Duare suffers her required allotments of abductions, she does an exemplary job of saving Carson's bacon on more than one occasion. In *Lost on Venus* she pulls Carson out of a cannibal barbecue *and* from the jaws of a hungry serpent. Plucky little gal, that Duare!

Now Carson was not the first Burroughs hero in need of rescuing. But in being snatched from the jaws of a serpent by a young girl—a one-eyed serpent at that—it seems that Burroughs is making more than just an off-color joke at Carson's expense. Carson is far from being the greatest swordsman of one world, let alone two. An attempt to be Tarzanic in *Lost on Venus* (battling barehanded an Amtorian bull) results in his undignified propulsion into a nearby tree. While the political satire of the Venus books is fairly straightforward with the communist Thorists of *Pirates* and the Nazi-like Zani of *Carson of Venus*, the Amtor saga also serves as a light-hearted parody of Burroughs's own work. Burroughs never wanted Carson to ape John Carter's heroics; he wanted Carson to be the polar opposite. John Carter declares his defiance of a hostile world with the challenge "I still live!" Carson changes this exclamatory declaration into a question when he remarks, "Each morning that I awoke on Venus it was with a sense of surprise that I still lived." There's more than one way to be heroic. Carson's heroism just involves getting the tar whupped out of him on a regular basis.[1]

1. Carson inexplicably develops a John-Carter-style chip on his shoulder and a certain moral smugness in *Escape on Venus* that has not been present before. When enslaved, Carson expects his captors to accord him the respect due a person of his station; when in battle, he takes delight in mowing the enemy down; in assessing the assorted nonhuman races that he encounters, he defines them as freaks of nature and of a lower

In our current politically correct climate, wherein we criticize our ignorant ancestors for not being as enlightened as we, much has been made of Burroughs's propensity for presenting white Anglo-Saxon males as the lords of creation. Tarzan will never be able to live down the fact that his name means "white skin." But by the 1930s Burroughs's Victorian notions of fine breeding and noble blood, which were part and parcel of so much of his fiction, had been dulled enough to be made fun of, again, at Carson's expense. Tarzan's "uncouth and savage training" could not eradicate his innate aristocratic bearing, something programmed into his genes. John Carter is a southern gentleman, a landed aristocrat with the fighting blood of Virginia coursing through his veins. Carson Napier comes from a seemingly good family—his parents were a British army officer and "an American girl from Virginia"—but he possesses something that would mortify any other Burroughs hero: bad blood.

Shortly after dropping into the tree city of Vepaja, Carson receives a blood test, the results of which show that his blood constitutes "a menace to the continued existence of human life on Amtor." Burroughs elaborates upon that joke more fully in *Lost on Venus*, wherein Carson stumbles upon the eugenic utopia of Havatoo. Here the social Darwinist prejudice toward fine breeding has been carried to a scientifically rational conclusion, the result being a beautiful city inhabited solely by beautiful people, a people who need no manmade laws because all citizens are conversant with the natural laws of proper human behavior. Carson is tested again, and this time he is revealed to "possess inherent psychological faults" and "inherited expressions, complexes, and fears." The decision is made that "it would best serve the interests of humanity" if Carson were destroyed. Carson finds it a tad unjust that he should die "simply because one of my ancestors failed to exercise a little intelligence in the selection of his bride." Burroughs does eventually tell us the name

social order. In short, Carson is a real jerk. The answer for this sudden character shift may be in the writing schedule Burroughs followed. Written in 1940, *Escape on Venus* comprises four novellas; he wrote them concurrently with the four novellas that compose the Mars adventure *Llana of Gathol* and the inner-world book *Savage Pellucidar*. Burroughs wrote one Venus story, one Mars story, and one Pellucidar story, and then started all over again until he had written twelve stories in all. This might have kept things interesting for Burroughs, but the result is three books that share a uniformity of plot, pacing, and characterization, none of them terribly successfully. *Escape on Venus* is bottom-of-the-barrel Burroughs.

of one of Carson's deficient ancestors: Deacon Edmund Rice, who by coincidence also happens to be an ancestor of Edgar Rice Burroughs.

Carson gets out of that scrape, of course, but you will just have to read that story to find out how. In the 1932 *Writer's Digest* article "The Tarzan Theme," Burroughs observed, "We would each like to be like Tarzan. At least I would; I admit it." That confession made, the Venus books suggest that if Burroughs ever found himself the hero of an interplanetary romance, he'd be Carson Napier. Carson Napier is no John Carter, but why would he want to be? Really, John Carter possesses the ability to astrally project himself to any planet at will, and when his princess is kidnapped and taken to Jupiter or one of the moons of Mars, he has to follow in a *spaceship*? It's time for the Warlord of Mars to rest his brawn and exercise his brain. If I had to throw in my lot with any Burroughs hero I would follow Carson Napier any day; chances are I would live longer.

SCOTT TRACY GRIFFIN

Glossary

Cast of Characters

Alzo—Olthar's mate.

Anoos—Traitorous spy charged by the captain of the *Sofal* with infiltrating the Soldiers of Liberty. As a result, Anoos is strangled by Zog.

Burroughs, Edgar Rice—Popular Tarzana-residing author contacted by Carson Napier, who seeks a publisher for his narrative of the adventures he encountered on Venus.

Byea—Vepajan woman liberated from the Thorists by Carson's privateers.

Carson, Judge John—A renowned and wealthy Virginian, the judge was Carson's maternal great-grandfather, with whom Carson lived for three years during his childhood. Upon adulthood, Carson used his inheritance from the judge to finance his interplanetary expedition.

Chand Kabi—Carson's Hindu tutor, who also taught the young boy telepathy and mentalism.

Danus—Vepaja's chief physician and surgeon and head of the college of medicine and surgery, he was Carson's tutor and mentor in the court of Mintep, for whom Danus was the personal physician and curator of the royal library.

Duare—Eighteen-year-old virgin daughter of Mintep, Jong of Vepaja. As Mintep's only heir, she represents the hopes of the entire nation; Carson falls in love with her at first sight.

Duran—Patriarch of the House of Zar, his family rescues Carson from a tongzan and later takes him in as a ward.

Gamfor—A hulking Thorist conscript, Gamfor is a former farmer who becomes one of Carson's trusted lieutenants in the Soldiers of Liberty.

Gridley, Jason—Tarzana neighbor and friend of Edgar Rice Burroughs, Gridley launches an expedition to Pellucidar to rescue the imprisoned Emperor Innes, as detailed in Burroughs's novel *Tarzan at the Earth's Core.*

Hodson, Captain—Policeman responsible for Burroughs's Tarzana beat.

Honan—Vepajan friend of Kamlot captured by the Thorists while defending Duare; Honan becomes one of Carson's inner circle in the Soldiers of Liberty.

Innes, David—Former Connecticut Yankee, now emperor of Pellucidar, Innes's story is told in Burroughs's seven Inner World novels.

Jeans, Sir James—Astronomer who theorized that Venus could not possibly support life. Napier's experiences debunk him.

Jerry—Burroughs's nurse, who warns the author of the delayed hallucinogenic effects of the narcotics used in his recent surgery.

Kamlot—Younger son of Duran and friend and companion of Carson, he too is shanghaied by the Thorists and helps Carson overrun and commandeer the *Sofal.*

Kiron—Formerly a member of the Vepajan Jong's Guard, Kiron revolted with the Thorists but was later conscripted as a sailor on the *Sofal* as discipline for insubordination. He becomes a key figure in Carson's Soldiers of Liberty.

Klufar—Venusian scientist who proposed the theory of the relativity of distance, reconciling discrepancies on the Venusian map by multiplying them by the square of minus one.

Kodj—Malcontent sailor on the *Sofal* who joined Carson's mutiny, but disputed Carson's elevation to Captain of the ship. Kodj was transferred to the *Sovong* for his dissension.

Mintep—Jong of Vepaja, father of Duare, the seven-hundred-year-old king presides over Carson's capture and later release into Vepajan society.

Moosko—Corpulent Thorist ongyan captured by Carson's privateers, Moosko uses his influence over the klangan to effect an escape with Vilor, also abducting Duare.

Napier, Carson—An American adventurer determined to be the first man on Mars, Napier uses his considerable inheritance to build a rocketship in Mexico. Because of errors in his calculations, he lands on Venus instead, launching the events of *Pirates of Venus.*

Olthar—Older son of Duran and brother of Kamlot.

Perry, Abner—Friend and cohort of David Innes, Perry was responsible for maintaining communication with the surface world via the "Gridley Wave," a radio wave named for its discoverer, Jason Gridley.

Rothmund, Ralph—Edgar Rice Burroughs's secretary and man Friday.

Tarzan—John Clayton, Lord Greystoke, a member of Jason Gridley's expedition to Pellucidar to rescue David Innes. Tarzan's further adventures are chronicled in a series of twenty-four novels by Burroughs.

Thor—Vepajan laborer and former criminal, a rebel who formed the communistic Thorist party and overthrew the Vepajan monarchy, forcing the royal court and the learned classes to flee the country and form a government in hidden exile.

Tofar—Official in the court of Mintep, Jong of Vepaja, Tofar conducted Carson's first audience with the king.

Vilor—A Thorist spy commissioned to steal the formula for the Vepajan longevity serum, Vilor was mistakenly captured by a Thorist raiding party, a fact that he used to convince Carson he is a native Vepajan. He later collaborates with Moosko and the klangan to kidnap Duare.

von Horst, Lieutenant—Popular young member of the *o–220* crew. Lost in Pellucidar, Von Horst's story is detailed in Burroughs's novel *Back to the Stone Age.*

Welsh, Jimmy—Carson Napier's best friend and trusted assistant in planning the mission to Mars.

Zar—Family clan of Duran, Olthar, and Kamlot.

Zog—A former Vepajan slave, strong, good-natured, but unintelligent, sentenced to death for killing a Thorist officer who struck him. Zog became one of Carson's trusted lieutenants in the Soldiers of Liberty.

Zuppner, Captain—Captain of the zeppelin, the *o–220*, on the inner-world mission to rescue David Innes.

Zuro—Duran's mate.

Flora & Fauna

antelope—Herd animals similar to exotic versions of terrestrial species.

basto—A large, belligerent, dangerous omnivore similar to a cross between an earthly bison and a wild boar. Stands about six feet tall at its massive shoulders with stocky, three-toed feet; a blue, elephant-like hide; nasty tusks; and short powerful horns sprouting from a curly-haired poll. The basto's flesh is considered a delicacy by Amtorians; in return, it considers them to be tasty morsels.

birds—Enormous Vepajan birds are mentioned by Carson.

cat—A catlike carnivore is spotted by Carson while it stalks the herbivores of Noobol.

grass—Amtorian grass is pale violet in color with blue and purple flowers. It grows profusely on the coastal hills and inland areas of Noobol.

herbivores—Similar in conformation to earthly plains browsers, these swift and agile beasts roam in herds.

targo—The giant spider of the Vepajan forests, the targo's webbing is an important commodity for the Vepajans.

tongzan—A puma-like arboreal carnivore with four hand-like feet, powerful fanged jaws, a single eye on a stalk, and two huge crab-like pincers projecting from its neck. This dangerous animal is striped red and yellow.

trees—Vepajan giants soar more than five thousand feet into the lower cloud envelope, from which they draw their moisture, and can attain a thickness of one thousand feet in diameter. The foliage is lavender, heliotrope, and violet in color.

Geography

Amtor—The Venusians' name for their world.

The Free Land of Thora—Thorists' misleading appellation for their country.

Karbol—"Cold Country," the polar region of Venus erroneously believed by Amtorian cartographers to form the outer ring of their concentric climates.

Kooaad—The primary tree city of Vepaja, home to the jong and his court.

Noobol—Amtorian continent infiltrated by seditious Thorists, with whom Moosko and Vilor plan to rendezvous after kidnapping Duare.

Pellucidar—The inner world, a prehistoric land that occupies our own hollow Earth. David Innes and Abner Perry discovered this land in their Iron Mole, as detailed by Burroughs in *At the Earth's Core* and six sequels.

Sari—Capitol of David Innes's Pellucidarian empire.

Strabol—"Hot Country," the equatorial region of Venus believed by Venusian cartographers to comprise a circular central territory in their disk-shaped world.

Tarzana—The southern California community founded by Burroughs, where he resided and worked.

Trabol—"Warm Country," the temperate zone of Venus, encompassing Vepaja, Thora, and part of Noobol.

Vepaja—Formerly one of Amtor's greatest empires, this civilization was overthrown by revolting criminals and lower classes, forcing the royal house and the learned classes to establish a hidden kingdom in the great trees of an island. This nation became Carson's adopted homeland.

Peoples & Tribes

Amtorians—The native human race of Venus, or Amtor.

angan—The birdmen of Venus, a race of dark-skinned, winged humanoids with low, receding foreheads; beak-like noses; small, close-set eyes; and flat, slightly pointed ears. They have a large, bird-like chest; elongated arms with long-fingered, heavily nailed hands; and narrow hips with short, stocky legs ending in taloned, three-toed feet. Tufts of feathers grow on their heads and loins, and they have a spreading tail. Batlike wings consist of a thin membrane supported by a bony framework; hollow bones lighten the load carried by the wings. They are of low intelligence, having neither initiative nor ambition, and will serve the will of whomever is their master.

nobargan—"Hairy men," primitive hairy tribesmen of Amtor. They are naked and armed with slings, which they use with deadly accuracy.

Thorans—Residents of the land of Thora, composed of the former Vepajan lower classes and other revolutionaries.

Thorists—Communistic political party founded by the ex-con Thor to overthrow Vepaja.

Vepajans—Natives of the advanced civilization Vepaja. A beautiful, healthy, athletic race with an advanced culture and superb medical care.

Miscellaneous Terms

angan—"Bird man" in the Amtorian tongue.
bar—"Hair" in Amtorian.
bol—"Country" in Amtorian.
fal—The verb "kill" in Amtorian.
gan—"Man" in Amtorian.
ganfal—"Criminal" in Amtorian (from the root words for man and kill).
jan—"Daughter" in Amtorian.
janjong—"Princess," or jong's daughter, in Amtorian.
Jodades—"Luck-to-you," the traditional Amtorian greeting.
jong—"King" in Amtorian.
joram—"Ocean" in Amtorian, believed to comprise the majority of unexplored Venusian territory.
kar—"Cold" in Amtorian.
kl—Amtorian prefix applied to plural words that begin with a vowel.
klangan—"Bird Men," plural.
klongyan—Plural for ongyans.
kloo—Amtorian prefix applied to plural words that begin with a noun.
klooganfal—"Criminals," plural.
kloonobargan—"Hairy men," plural.
kung—The letter "k" in the Amtorian tongue.
Kung Kung Kung—"KKK," the acronym for Napier's Soldiers of Liberty mutineers.
lor—Venusian substance used to create energy via atomic reaction.
no—Amtorian contraction of "not" (their word for "with"), analogous to the English suffix "y" as in nobar, "hairy."
nobar—"Hairy" in Amtorian.
nobargan—"Hairy Man," a savage tribesman in Amtorian.
not—"With" in Amtorian.
notar—"Ship" in Amtorian.
ong—"Great" in Amtorian (by inference).
ongyan—"Great Friend," a title of eminence among the Thorists. One hundred klongyan rule Thora for their own gain.
R-ray—A deadly ray created by the reaction of two elements. It is harnessed in weapons used to dissolve human and animal tissue.
Ra jodades—Amtorian response to the greeting "Jodades."
ro—The number "three" in Amtorian.

san—The number "five" in Amtorian.

So—Amtorian prefix equivalent to the English suffix "er."

Sofal—"Killer," the Thorist ship to which Carson and Kamlot were abducted, which they then commandeered via mutiny.

Soldiers of Liberty—Carson's band of mutineers, also known by their Amtorian acronym, Kung Kung Kung.

Sovong—"Defender," the Thorist ship to which Duare was abducted.

stra—"Hot" in Amtorian.

T-ray—A deadly ray that will dissolve any substance. It is created with the radiation from Element 93 (vik-ro) reacting with Element 97. The ray is used in Thorist ray guns.

Tarel—The strong silken webbing of the targo, gathered by the Vepajans for a variety of uses.

te—Amtorian unit of time roughly analogous to the earthly hour but 80.895 minutes long. There are 20 te in the 26 hour, 56 minute, and 4 second Venusian day.

Thorism—Gospel of class hatred preached by the insurrectionist Thor in order to overthrow the Vepajan government.

tob—Amtorian unit of weight roughly equal to one-third pound. It is the standard unit of the Amtorian decimal system.

tork—Favorite Amtorian game, similar to poker but using pieces like those of earthly Mah Jong.

tra—"Warm" in Amtorian.

vik—The number "nine" in Amtorian.

vik-ro—Element 93, undiscovered on Earth at the time of Carson's adventure. This element reacts with yor-san (Element 105), contained in the substance lor. The resulting atomic reaction releases a tremendous quantity of energy, which is used to power Amtorian ships.

vong—The verb "defend" in Amtorian.

voo—Amtorian article translated as "the" or "a."

vookor—"Captain" in the Amtorian tongue.

Yan—"Friend," Moosko's ship.

yor—Amtorian term for the number "100."

yorsan—"Element 105" in Amtorian.

0–220—Zeppelin commanded by Gridley and Zuppner on their inner world mission.

In the Bison Frontiers of Imagination series

The Wonder
By J. D. Beresford
Introduced by Jack L. Chalker

At the Earth's Core
By Edgar Rice Burroughs
Introduced by Gregory A. Benford
Afterword by Phillip R. Burger

Beyond Thirty
By Edgar Rice Burroughs
Introduced by David Brin
Essays by Phillip R. Burger and Richard A. Lupoff

The Land That Time Forgot
By Edgar Rice Burroughs
Introduced by Mike Resnick

Pirates of Venus
By Edgar Rice Burroughs
Introduced by F. Paul Wilson
Afterword by Phillip R. Burger

The Poison Belt: Being an Account of Another Amazing Adventure of Professor Challenger
Sir Arthur Conan Doyle
Introduced by Katya Reimann

Omega: The Last Days of the World
By Camille Flammarion
Introduced by Robert Silverberg

Ralph 124C 41+
By Hugo Gernsback
Introduced by Jack Williamson

Mizora: A World of Women
By Mary E. Bradley Lane
Introduced by Joan Saberhagen

Before Adam
By Jack London
Introduced by Dennis L. McKiernan

Fantastic Tales
By Jack London
Edited by Dale L. Walker

The Moon Pool
By A. Merritt
Introduced by Robert Silverberg

The Purple Cloud
By M. P. Shiel
Introduced by John Clute

The Skylark of Space
By E. E. "Doc" Smith
Introduced by Vernor Vinge

The Chase of the Golden Meteor
By Jules Verne
Introduced by Gregory A. Benford

In the Days of the Comet
By H. G. Wells
Introduced by Ben Bova

The Last War: A World Set Free
By H. G. Wells
Introduced by Greg Bear

The Sleeper Awakes
By H. G. Wells
Introduced by J. Gregory Keyes
Afterword by Gareth Davies-Morris

When Worlds Collide
By Philip Wylie and Edwin Balmer
Introduced by John Varley